A Poisonwood & Lyric Novella

POISONWOOD

Sam Burns
W.M. Fawkes

FlickerFox
Books

Content Warning: this book is intended for adult audiences only, and contains graphic violence, swearing, and graphic sex scenes. Includes inadvertent self-harm, self-neglect, poisoning.

Cover art © 2020 by Natasha Snow Designs; www.natashasnowdesigns.com
Editing by Clause & Effect

JASPER

J asper had never been hungrier, and the city of Lyric was full to the brink of tantalizing life. There were indie musicians hitting the pavement, hoping to be discovered playing in dive bars and willing to settle on a different kind of attention, hedge fund managers who desperately needed to unwind, people looking for someone to fill a void or entertain them for a night. He could smell sex everywhere, and it was killing him.

He stood in the kitchen, his arms crossed, wondering if the seals around the apartment's windows and doors were broken. Alluring as Lyric's citizens were, the urge to run out into the night and cut a hot, sweaty path through sex-starved mortals shouldn't be so strong.

"Thirsty?" a female voice asked behind him.

His sister Sasha wrapped her arm around his shoulder and swung around to his front, nearly toppling them both over. A demon at his best wouldn't even notice the weight of spritely Sasha, but a starving incubus was weaker than a human. He only caught himself when she gracefully landed on the balls of her feet, and he could steady by leaning on her.

With a self-deprecating laugh, Jasper rubbed the back of his neck. "Sorry. Caught me off guard there, sis."

She arched one thick black brow at him. "Did I?" Then, she was on him again, in his space. That was the thing about incubi —they were touchers. In the decade since his demon side had woken, he'd adjusted to it. Hell, it was nice most of the time. He still flinched back when she touched his forehead. "How are you feeling? You look pale."

"I'm fine," Jasper said.

Sasha pursed her dusty pink lips. Though she was his sister, it was only on their father's side. They didn't look much alike. Her skin was a beautiful cool brown, her eyes so dark they were nearly black, with natural hair she kept shaved tight on the sides that spilled in a waterfall of curls from the top.

All incubi were blessed with good looks and more than their fair share of grace, but Sasha could've been a dancer, the way she swung around him.

Jasper wasn't half as impressive.

"You're not eating enough," Sasha accused.

Sexual conquest was a point of pride for their kind, but Jasper grew less and less comfortable with the prospect every day. On the news every morning, there were reports of awful people who took without asking, women and men and folks of every sort who suffered because monstrous people thought they had a right to use someone else for their own pleasure. How was that any different from what incubi did to survive? As he'd gotten older, the thrill of the hunt was less appealing. He could understand why Declan avoided it.

If their father caught him not eating, he'd have starved Jasper to prove how much he'd miss it. He might've disowned him like he'd done to Declan. But Sasha reached for his hand and squeezed softly.

"Listen, I know it's not always simple, but we don't *force* them, Jasper. People come to us. They want to. It's not like we don't give them anything back."

Jasper flinched. Yeah, people came to them, because incubi were magnetic. Humans didn't have much choice in the matter. He'd learned that lesson all too well when he was in high school. Puberty hit hard—all of the sudden, he had lean abs, people smiled at him in the hallways between classes, and his straight best friend shoved him against the wall under the stairwell and felt him up.

It'd sucked, not because he didn't want Luke to touch him— he'd wanted that more than anything. But he'd been fifteen. The first time he'd come with anyone, it was grinding through their clothes under the stairwell until they both had wet boxers. And Luke . . . afterward, Luke hadn't been able to look at him.

He hadn't wanted it, and because of what Jasper was, Luke hadn't been able to help himself.

Jasper's father found him soon after that. It was a relief, at least, to have his questions answered, but he had never figured out how to balance what he needed with what was right.

Increasingly, he was sure that there was no way to be both a demon and a decent person.

"I'm eating plenty," Jasper promised, squeezing her hand back.

"Did I hear that twinkubus is thirsty?" Malcolm joined them in the kitchen. The three of them, the youngest children of Elrith, shared a top-floor penthouse in one of Lyric's finest high-rises. Their brother Declan lived across the hall. But they had other siblings—no doubt more than Jasper knew.

"You coming out with us tonight?" Malcolm asked, swinging his arm over Sasha's shoulder.

Jasper's mouth went dry. It would be so easy to go out, find someone, and lose himself for a few hours. Guilt would come later, but he was so fucking hungry *now*. "I don't think so," he rasped. "Is Declan coming?"

Sasha shook her head. No surprise there. Declan rarely went out, but it would've been nice to keep company with someone as uncomfortable as Jasper.

Malcolm rolled his eyes. As always, the gray slacks and white button up he wore were immaculately pressed. They were plain, but screamed wealth. No one liked being an incubus quite as much as Malcolm did. He rolled his sleeves up, checked his smartwatch, and shrugged. "Your call, bro, but I'm ready to go. Sasha?"

She gave Jasper an uneasy smile and shrugged. "Girl's gotta eat, Jas. You sure you don't want to come?"

Jasper shook his head. He couldn't talk, or his tongue might betray him. It might be best if he could learn how not to breathe.

Again, she touched his arm, like that would fix all this. "Okay."

Malcolm turned away, but Sasha hung back, staring at him until Jasper's grin began to feel stretched and unnatural. Should he say he was fine again?

"Listen, I . . . have this friend. A witch," she said softly, digging in her purse for her phone. "She's got a store, and—I don't know. I think you should talk to her."

A moment later, Jasper's phone buzzed. He pulled it out of his pocket and opened the contact Sasha had sent him. "Poppy Silverstone?"

"Yeah. I think she can help you."

"Sasha," Malcolm called from the entryway. "The party train is leaving. If you're not on it, you're on your own."

Sasha bounced up on her toes and kissed Jasper once on each cheek. "Try and have a good night. Watch something on Netflix. Maybe Declan's in. Love you."

"Love you too," he said, still staring at the contact on his phone's screen and the address for a store: Silverstone's Emporium.

Jasper supposed, if breathing was still critical and he couldn't escape the pheromones everywhere, he'd try anything. When they opened in the morning, he'd go.

Until then, he had a date with his television and a pint of mint chocolate chip—the second best thing to sex.

2

CALEB

Caleb didn't want to get out of bed.

At the beginning of winter, it always felt decadent and a little naughty, spending more and more time in bed. He'd get up, stoke the fire and make himself some hot chocolate, then curl up under the blanket and stay there.

By February, he just didn't feel like moving. It wasn't decadent. There was no chocolate. It felt like too damn much work to get up and put a log on the fire, and the only reason he did that was because if he didn't, he'd have to light the damn thing over again, which was more work.

That, in fact, was the only reason he got out of bed. It was still damn cold outside, and he wasn't going to freeze to death from sheer laziness.

It was just . . . he was starting to wonder why not.

He'd moved out into the woods to be alone, sure. He didn't like most people, fine. Who did?

But as much of a misanthrope as he was, Caleb was lonely. He didn't want to move back to the city and pretend to like people again or anything, it would just be nice if he had someone to talk to. Someone to snuggle up with him under the blanket all winter.

Maybe then it wouldn't be so hard to care when spring came.

There was a sharp knock at the door, and he cringed.

Sure, he was alone, but he knew that knock and it was company he could do without. "Go away, witch."

"I'm not a witch, I'm—"

"Yes, you are, and I don't know why you persist in saying you're my wife when I tell you to go away." He pulled the blanket over his head, like that would get rid of her. "It's creepy."

"Oh, for—watch a movie sometime, ya dink. *The Princess Bride* is a classic. You're as bad as the monster you're neighbors with. And open up, I'm freezing my ass off out here." She knocked again, as though he'd have forgotten where the door was in the meantime.

She always mentioned the Poisonwood monster whenever she was annoyed about him being antisocial, like he was going to turn into a monster himself if he didn't go clubbing. He sighed and got out of bed, dragging himself over to the door and opening it just far enough to admit one tiny annoying witch. Then he tromped back over to his bed and pulled the blanket over himself again.

"Really?" she asked, sounding irritated already. "You answer the door in your underwear, don't even offer me a drink, and you've let your fire go out?"

"I'm not under a hospitality geas," he retorted. "It's my house. I'm allowed to be in my underwear. You know where the water is—get it yourself if you want it. If you're going to compare me to a feral forest spirit, I might as well act like one. And . . ."

"And?"

"I didn't feel like getting up."

There was a sharp snap, and the room filled with warmth a second later. "You're absolutely the worst, Caleb."

"Funny, I don't remember coming to your house in the middle of your hibernation and demanding you see to my needs." Giving up on getting back to sleep, he whipped the blanket down and glared at her. "What do you want?"

"First of all," she said, and held her fingers up like she was going to make a list. Oh gods, she was going to make a list. "This is not the middle of your hibernation, dillhole. It's spring. You should be out catching salmon or whatever it is you do when you need to fatten yourself up again."

"I'm still tired."

"You're not."

"Then explain why I'm trying to sleep?" He sat up and threw his legs over the side of the bed. The floor was still icy cold, even though she'd restarted the fire as a near inferno, and he almost pulled his feet back up. "Better yet, explain why you're keeping me from sleeping."

She looked down at her fingers blankly for a moment like she was trying to remember the next item on her list, then shrugged it off. "You're done hibernating. Winter is over. And I swear, if you tell me winter is coming . . ."

"Winter is always coming."

She pulled off a mitten and threw it at his head. "It's time to get up and get back to life, Caleb. No more hiding from the world and sleeping all the time."

"I'm a bear, it's what I do."

"Again, it's spring. For fuck's sake, at least get up and watch some TV." She waved at the dusty television hanging on the wall in front of the equally dusty couch.

"I don't watch TV."

She put her head in her hands. "I swear, Caleb. You're a bear, not a stick in the mud. Stop acting like one. I got you a satellite dish specifically so you'd have other people in your life, even if they were fictional." She marched over to his refrigerator and opened it up, groaning again. "And go to the grocery store. Or catch some fish or gather some berries or whatever it is you came out to the middle of nowhere to do. Just do something. I'm begging you."

At that, he gave up, pulled his feet into the bed, drew the blanket up again, and rolled over so his back was facing her. "Go away, Poppy."

With grim and heavy satisfaction, he heard her growl and stomp out, slamming the door of his cabin behind her.

3

JASPER

Somehow, Jasper survived the night on his own. He was still awake, staring hollow-eyed at the TV screen, when Sasha returned, obviously debauched. She hooked her fingers to dangle her heels in her hand, and her hair was flat in the back. Her cheeks were flushed, her skin had a healthy glow, and when she smiled, she had the kind of beauty that men fought over. Most of the time, being an incubus sucked, but Jasper had family now—messy, sometimes problematic family, but he loved them. Usually.

"Lost Malcolm?" he asked.

Sasha laughed. "I don't think he'll be back until tomorrow."

They all hunted differently—Jasper was tentative and awkward, Sasha was efficient and clean and made quick escapes, and Malcolm was self-indulgent. He liked to preen and be petted all night long. Declan, alone, did not hunt at all. Rather, he called a service and never booked the same person twice.

"And did you have a good night?"

"Great night," she said. He was glad she didn't elaborate. The last thing he needed was to think about sex.

"Good."

"Yeah," she agreed, dropping her heels by the door and crossing the hardwood floor on light feet. "I'm gonna snag a shower. Get some rest, Jas." She'd squeezed his shoulder on the way past.

He listened to the water running through the pipes overhead, his thoughts distant and foggy. When he'd been human, he remembered saying he'd kill for a taco. He hadn't meant it, but that was how it felt now—he would do absolutely anything to feel full again. And that made him dangerous.

Jasper turned up the television and sank down into the couch, dragging a blanket around him. It smelled like incubus— not at all appealing.

After he heard Sasha turn the shower off and drop into bed in the next room over, Jasper didn't go to his own room. He might be able to sleep on the couch, with a cartoon sitcom about a depressed horse playing in the background, but if he went to his own bed and laid alone in the silence, he had no chance. He turned the volume down so it wouldn't bother her, and curled up with his head on the arm rest.

In the morning, getting up was just a matter of rolling off the couch, changing his wrinkled clothes, and brushing his teeth. He'd hardly slept at all.

But Sasha said Poppy at Silverstone's Emporium could help. He trusted her; he had to. He didn't think he could keep on like this, and he sure didn't have the stomach left to feed the way his siblings did. If he fed from someone, he wanted to know they wanted him too, and there was just no way to tell if that was sincere.

The emporium's website said they opened at ten a.m. With nowhere else to be on a Sunday morning, Jasper got there early. He parked the flashy yellow Tesla his father had bought him for his last birthday on a side street, fed the meter, and made his way around the block to peer in the window.

Generally speaking, most humans weren't aware of the paranormal underground that slithered all around them. Silverstone's Emporium was a little hole-in-the-wall shop that from the outside, seemed catered to the humans who bought into the new-age idea that if you rubbed the right crystal on your face, it would solve all your skin problems.

Shit, Jasper wasn't being fair. Incubi didn't get sick, didn't get pimples, and could hide any flaws behind a glamour. Whatever humans did to make themselves feel better and cared for was worthwhile. A witch could sell them a special rock (with an even more special enchantment) and make a buck while their human clientele remained none the wiser. What did it matter how the thing worked, so long as it did? He was just in a sour fucking mood.

At nine-forty-five, Jasper paced in front of Silverstone's window. Five minutes later, he leaned in to inspect the wares, wrapping his jacket tighter around his middle. There were shops like this in most cities, he guessed. Even if humans couldn't see the magic around them, they wanted to believe it was there. Hell,

Jasper had wanted to believe in magic too, before it'd hit him in the face like a sack of bricks, landing him with pointed horns, a spiked tale, and creepy glowing demon eyes.

Okay, he didn't have to show those off all the time, but going from thinking you were a normal (or normal-adjacent) kid to sprouting goddamn horns was an entire fucking journey.

Nine-fifty-two, and one of the commuters on the sidewalk stopped in his tracks a few feet from Jasper. Freezing in place, Jasper turned to see the man staring at him, pupils dilated. Since he'd decided not to feed, Jasper'd rarely left their penthouse. It occurred to him there on the sidewalk that the pheromones he put off must've been overwhelming. Most people looked hungrily at him and moved on—it usually took some small effort on an incubi's part to coax a person in as their desire warred with their instinctual fear of demons.

But this guy stopped and watched him. When he approached, it was with a predatory grin. "Hey, kid."

Jasper fought the urge to grimace, twisting it instead into a smile. "Hello."

"You want to get out of here? Find somewhere quiet?" His eyes darted left, toward an alley in the center the block. Gross.

Jasper frowned. "Like that alley? Maybe a dingy hotel?"

The man nodded. He licked his chapped lips. He was handsome enough—average looking and clean-cut with a body a little soft from sitting in a desk most of the time. Jasper usually liked that—when bodies were soft, or had scars, or weren't carved specifically for the purposes of hunting down sexual partners. But the whole point was not taking advantage, and this guy didn't know what he was doing. Or if he did, that was every bit as bad.

"No," Jasper said firmly. "Thank you though."

Jasper turned back to the window. The guy stepped in and reached for his arm. His fingers, short but firm, dug into the hollow of Jasper's elbow. "Let's get out of here," he growled.

Jasper jerked his arm back. He might be the least of Elrith's sons and a poor excuse for an incubus, but he was still a demon, not some kid to be shoved around by a random corporate-drone passerby.

"I said no," Jasper snapped. "Now move along."

The guy hesitated, weighing his options, so Jasper flashed a little fang, let his eyes glow red, and he scurried away. When Jasper composed himself in the window's reflection, he was flushed, wide-eyed. His breath escaped him in a low, steady flow as he watched his shoulders sink. He wanted this to be over.

Ten o'clock hit, and the store didn't open. He didn't see anyone shuffling around within. Frowning, he checked the door to be sure. Maybe it unlocked magically.

No such luck.

Ten o'five, and he tried calling. Nobody picked up.

And then, at ten o'seven, he leaned into the door with both hands cupped to block out the light from the street, and someone behind him cleared her throat.

"Hi," she chirped.

He spun, staring down at her. She was a petite, round-cheeked woman with a halo of dark curls. Her skirt was purple—

more a patchwork of scarves than anything truly sewn. She had a silver ring on every finger.

"So *sorry* to keep you waiting." The way she spoke, the timbre of her voice floating up and down as if completely untethered, made it hard to focus on what she was saying. Or, you know, maybe he was starving. "Poppy Silverstone, at your service."

She stuck out her hand. Dazed, he took it and shook. "Uh, Jasper Jones."

Poppy clicked her tongue. "Unfortunate."

Jasper shrugged. "Not as bad as Malcolm McKittack, but I get what you mean." As soon as he'd learned what alliteration was in seventh grade, it'd bugged him. Felt silly. But Jones was his mother's name—the only one he'd had any right to until he'd hit puberty—and by that point, it'd felt like his name was, well, his name.

Then his mom had died, and her name was how he could hold onto her. He'd thought, for a while, that it'd help him hold onto his humanity too, but no dice there.

Malcolm was the only one of Elrith's kids—well, that Jasper knew—who'd changed his name. Malcolm McKittack was the name of a special kind of douche, though. Jasper Jones had grown on him.

Letting go of Poppy's hand, he stuck his in his jacket pockets. "I'm Sasha Washington's brother. She, uh, she said you might be able to help me."

With pursed lips, Poppy looked him over. Then, she dug out her keys and opened the door. "You'd better come inside if we're going to talk about *your* kind of problem."

He followed her in, shutting the door. With all the purple satin curtains hanging everywhere, the whole place was shadowy and strange. It reeked of bergamot and incense.

"So, what's the problem? Stopped up? Overzealous? Food all going to ash in your mouth? You know, it's not uncommon for incubi to lose interest in regular food after—"

"It's not that," Jasper croaked. He raked his hand through his hair and rubbed the back of his neck. His head felt warm and floaty, like a hot air balloon. Shit, this was harder than he'd thought it'd be. "I, uh . . . I'm—I'm not up for, you know, *feeding*." By the end, his voice fell to a whisper.

Behind the counter, Poppy frowned. She crossed her arms. The little pucker between her brows was downright adorable.

"So you're feeling weak? How long's it been?"

"A month?"

Poppy blinked, her eyes so wide he could see the whites around her light green irises. Still, shock wasn't judgment. "And before that?"

"Another month?"

"Is it—" She bit her lip. At least he wasn't the only one awkward about it. "Is it because you *can't*, or—"

"I just don't want to? Well, it's not that I don't *want* to, but I don't want to make anybody—and there's no—no way to not . . . Well, it's like having sex with someone who's drunk. It's not consensual. They don't—can't—know what they want. I—I can't keep doing . . ." He shrugged and stared down at the glass counter full of baubles between them. Fuck if he wasn't already the worst person in the world.

"Okay." Poppy leaned forward, her arms crossed under her chest. "First off, it's not like you're a vampire or anything. Some people say everybody should try having sex with an incubus at least once in their lives."

Jasper grimaced, shrinking down into his shoulders. The exchange of commodity wasn't much better. Everything boiled down to sex, and he wanted . . . he wanted someone to have feelings for him that weren't based on pheromones and glamour. Did wanting some kind of genuine intimacy make him a bad incubus? He knew what Elrith would've said to that. No point asking.

"Have you thought about hiring a sex worker?" Poppy asked. "I mean, Sasha says Elrith's got all kinds of cash to throw around. And isn't that what your brother Declan does?"

His dad was a big man in the demon community. He made deals and got shit done. Elrith had more money than the Catholic church, and he was loose with it, which left an awful lot of freedom for Jasper to hide out and eat ice cream. Wasn't all bad.

But he couldn't imagine his father's face if he said he wanted to hire a sex worker. Respectable incubi didn't need to *pay* to feed. That was why he and Declan had had their falling out. And, again— "I don't think that's for me. I just don't want to be hungry. That's it. Can you help with that?"

Poppy's lips twisted to the side and she shrugged. "Not really? Well, not *here*, but I might know of one thing that can help you." With one cocked finger, she beckoned him closer. "So you're sure you want an out? Want to feel full without the rat race?"

Jasper leaned across the counter. Catching her eye, he nodded. "Definitely."

"Okay. So there's a yellow flower that grows in the Poison-wood Forest at the base of Grandmother Mountain. If you find it and eat it, you'll have guilt-free sustenance forever. Won't have to seduce an unwitting human again."

"Really?" Jasper's smile grew. It couldn't be that easy. If it were, why wasn't everyone taking it?

Hells gates, he did not want to ponder the answer to that too hard. Couldn't be that they liked feeding that much.

"Really. Silverstone honor." She held up two fingers. "Give me your phone."

She did a quick Google search and took a screenshot of an unfamiliar yellow blossom—to be fair, Jasper didn't know much about wildflowers—and handed it back to him.

"That's what you're looking for."

"Thank you," Jasper breathed. "Thank you so much, Poppy."

"Any time, kiddo." She flashed him a bright grin. "Good luck munching grass."

He was out the door by ten-fifteen and back in his car. A hike through the woods was harder than picking something up at the store, but it was an answer. Even if Jasper wasn't the most outdoorsy guy around, he could manage a walk. After he got a new pair of hiking boots.

THE STORE CLERK had assured him that Timberlands were the

very best for a mountain hike, and Jasper wasn't taking any chances. He even stopped by the park's service station to pick up a map of the Poisonwood Forest and the trails around Grandmother Mountain in case he lost signal.

But two hours into his hike, and he worried he was lost anyway. Who the hell thought looking at a thing on a map from above was the same as actually standing in the middle of a bunch of freaking trees? His phone had a compass, which gave him a vague sense of wrongness he wasn't sure how to fix, and other than that, it was totally useless.

If he could find high enough ground, he could at least see the mountain, so he kept marching up, and up. The arches of his feet cramped, and he realized the jeans he'd worn were way too tight for climbing. That, and the cold tickled his exposed knee where they'd been ripped by the manufacturer.

Still, he could pull this off. He had to. Then, everything would be great. He'd . . . he'd never sleep with anyone again. That kind of sucked, but at least he wouldn't be hurting anybody. He could totally live with that. Totally.

It wasn't until he got up a particularly steep bit that he saw, on a hillside beneath him, a scattering of yellow flowers, right there in what would've been his path if he'd kept on walking.

He scrambled back down the rock face and crouched in front of them. They smelled vaguely sweet, their blossoms small in the early spring.

And they'd fix everything.

They were maybe the most perfect flowers ever.

Jasper plucked one off of its stem and shoved it into his mouth. He chewed, swallowed, gave it a minute.

He didn't feel anything change. He was still starving, so fucking hungry. This had to work.

So he ate another. Then he ate five more.

And then his stomach began to cramp.

He hadn't felt pain like that since before he'd become a demon. His stomach roiled, churning and angry, and Jasper gasped. For a moment, he thought he was going to puke, but his throat was too tight. Swollen shut. He was sweating hard.

This was all wrong. He jerked his phone out of his pocket and dialed Sasha.

But he had no signal. The call failed, and he tipped forward and fell on his face on a hill of wildflowers.

4

CALEB

The salmon weren't exactly jumping yet, but there were enough for Caleb to catch a dozen easily. It took him most of the day, but at least if he caught fish, he didn't have to go into town and go to the grocery store.

He probably should anyway. He wasn't an actual bear, after all. Nuts and berries and salmon were all well and good, but a man needed hot chocolate to live. Some eggs would be good, too, and he didn't keep chickens. He wouldn't have a clue where to start, and his bearish nature would probably scare the things to death anyway.

Line of fish hung over one shoulder, he turned back toward his cabin. The path back was circuitous. He didn't want to wander straight through the lair of the local corrupted forest spirit, but it was still only a few miles.

The salmon were sign enough, he supposed, that it was spring. Even if his heart didn't feel like spring, it had arrived.

Grasses were growing, leaves were unfurling on the deciduous trees, and flowers were blooming.

Also, it was newbie hiker season. They wandered off the trails, up into the woods, got lost, and sometimes died of exposure or starvation.

Or sometimes, as in the case of the body Caleb almost tripped over, the damned ignorant walnuts ate poisonous flowers. Like the bright yellow color had been a lure and not a deterrent, the man still had one clutched in his hand.

Caleb rolled his eyes and pulled his phone out of his pocket to see if he could get a signal for a ranger to come pick up the body, but then the guy pulled in a deep wheezing breath, and Caleb almost dropped his phone.

He fell to his knees next to the man, fish forgotten, and checked his pulse. High and thready, but still there. He must be a supernatural creature of some kind, to have survived eating one at all.

Well, that changed things. Caleb piled his line of fish on the guy's chest—What? He wasn't going to leave them there; he'd worked hard for those—and picked the man up in a princess carry.

Back at his cabin, he dropped the fish on the kitchen counter for cleaning, and took the guy into the bedroom. Not that there was really a bedroom, it was more one big open area, and Caleb thought of the part with the giant bed and the sheepskin rug as his bedroom.

He took off the guy's fishy shirt, tossed it into the wash, and set the man on his bed. Also, he wasn't going to have anyone get dirt in his bed, so he pulled off his shoes and socks. Brand new hiking boots. Frack, the guy had blisters on his heels. Had he even been hiking before today? Stripped down to his fashionable ripped blue jeans, the guy looked more like the victim of a night of debauchery than of self-poisoning.

He was absolutely beautiful too. Long golden-blond hair, fine-boned features that looked almost fae, and an impressive set of abs. Probably spent half his time lifting weights.

After checking again to make sure the man was breathing, Caleb sighed bitterly and turned to his cupboard. He finally got a beautiful man into his bed, and of course, it was just because he'd been poisoned.

Sure, Caleb didn't exactly spend a lot of time seeking out bed partners, but that was just depressing. Just like most things lately, he supposed.

He scavenged his cupboards and found what he needed for a simple remedy. Unless the guy was a vampire, Caleb could have the poison cured soon enough. And if he were a vampire, he'd already be dead, what with wandering out in the sun.

Throwing all the right herbs in the pot with water, he covered it and let it simmer while he went to clean the fish. The guy was going to need some food when he came around, after all. Even if he lived through it, poisoning was hard on a body.

It didn't take long to clean and prepare the fish and then throw together a pot of chowder. By the time he was done, the remedy was ready. He strained the woody bits out, and, glancing over at the unconscious man, threw in some sugar syrup.

It didn't exactly taste bad, but . . . Okay, no, it tasted terrible, and a man who wore brand new hiking boots, got blisters, and proceeded to eat one of the only poisonous varieties of plant in the local forest didn't seem like the kind of man who would do well with that. It had nothing to do with him being beautiful. Or with Caleb being worried about the kind of man who would do a thing like that.

After all, there was always the chance it hadn't been an accident.

It would be a strange way to kill oneself, but not unheard of. He hoped the cute little twink wasn't trying to kill himself. Sure, Caleb was basing his opinion off looks, but it was all he had to go by. The guy was cute, and he didn't immediately seem like an asshole. At least he'd bought the boots and not tried to go hiking in loafers or something like that.

And, of course, Caleb was lonely. He hated himself for it a little, but he wanted the guy to be someone nice.

Not that he wouldn't have saved an asshole. Probably.

He sat down on his bed and shifted the guy half into his lap, angling him up a bit so he could pour the remedy down his throat. It took some effort, and he could only get one mouthful down at a time, but slowly, as he worked, color came back into the twink's adorable rosy cheeks, and his breathing and heart rate steadied.

When his beautiful blue-gray eyes fluttered open, Caleb sighed in relief, and not at all in wistful longing. He wasn't that pathetic, no matter what Poppy said.

5

JASPER

He wasn't dead. When he'd fallen onto the forest floor, his useless cell phone clutched in one hand and a yellow flower in the other, Jasper had expected not to wake up again. As his body chilled and his thoughts became gossamer wisps that floated away, he figured it was just as well. He was an incubus who couldn't eat; best to die like this than starving slow. And best to die than hurt somebody else.

But then he didn't die. That awareness returned to him in stages—first the bittersweet taste in his mouth, then a heat pressed against his side, under one leg. Warmer, still, because it pressed into his skin directly. His shirt was gone, and someone sat behind him, breathing, a slow and steady rumble that Jasper felt inside his own ribcage.

Jasper opened his eyes on a man with a gorgeous jawline who smelled like sweet beard oil and smoke and . . . fish? His nose scrunched up.

The man's breath huffed through his nose. "It doesn't taste the best, but it's a mite better than poison."

"Poison?" Jasper croaked. His throat was sore, rough from coughing and whatever was in the cup the man had held to his lips.

"So you didn't mean to eat those flowers?" There was a concerned furrow to the man's dark brow. His face was square and serious, his beard thick—but not quite thick enough to obscure the fullness of his frowning lips. Jasper felt a little like he'd been caught at sixteen, sneaking in after a night of drinking, but he didn't think Elrith would've cared this much.

"I—I did," Jasper admitted with a grimace.

The stranger flinched, a rigid line against his side. His scowl darkened. Gently, he moved Jasper off him.

"You should eat something." It was there, in the glint of his eyes and the man's easy strength—this stranger wasn't human. Or not quite.

The man got up, turning his back to him. Holy hell, he had to be twice as broad as Jasper, thick with muscle only obscured by a worn plaid flannel and practical jeans that looked like he could move around in them. Not like Jasper's, plastered to his legs, that'd made scrambling over rocks a pain. He worried the hole on his thigh had gone from artful to blown out for his efforts.

There, at the counter of a kitchen on the far side of the room, the man ladled something into a bowl. Jasper felt the weight of his disappointment.

And what did he care for some lumberjack wanna-be's disappointment in him, anyway? He hadn't done anything. And still, an explanation tumbled out of his mouth before he could think better of it.

"I meant to eat them. But I didn't mean to, uh, poison myself. I, um—well, my sister sent me to this witch, see, and she said that yellow flower could fix—fix me." Jasper stumbled over the end, his voice breaking, chewing his lip. He hung his head, shrugged his shoulders, and scooted back against the guy's pillows. When he sat up, it was almost like he was in control. Well, until he looked too closely at the man's broad, rough hands. Those were the hands of a man who actually knew what control meant.

This was the guy's bed. His scent was all over it. Jasper was in some random guy's bed, half undressed, and *not* thoroughly fucked.

Something was wrong with that. Jasper was still starving—the flowers hadn't done shit. Humans on the street couldn't help gawking at him. And this guy was scowling and ladling soup, completely unbothered.

He came back over, holding the bowl out of Jasper's reach.

"What do you mean, fix you?"

Jasper's shoulders jerked up. "Personal."

The man grunted and nodded. "Fair enough. Can you promise not to spill a drop of this in my bed?"

Jasper nodded. Already, he was pushing himself to get up though. No reason to make the guy uncomfortable. "I can—"

A huge, warm, callused hand came down on his bare shoulder and held him still. "You need to rest."

Staring up at him, Jasper swallowed. He nodded slowly, and

when he sank back into the pillows, the man passed him the bowl. "Eat."

Starving was starving, and even if soup wasn't going to do much for his incubus problems, the command to stuff his face was convincing. Jasper took a bite. It was peppery and salty and rich. "It's good. Thanks. I'm Jasper Jones."

"Caleb."

"Nice to meet you, Caleb."

Caleb continued to watch him, but it wasn't in the hungry, calculating way Jasper had come to expect. There were some things about his nature he couldn't control, and his body wanted to survive even if he had moral quandaries with *how*. He should've been putting off enough pheromones to bring a guy as big as Caleb to his knees.

But something was broken. He could look Caleb over, imagine the strength of the arm that'd been wrapped around his shoulders only minutes before, and then meet those hazel eyes flecked with amber, and nothing happened. Caleb didn't knock the bowl out of his hands, cover him with his enormous body, and fuck him down into the mattress.

He should have. Why wasn't he trying?

What should've been a relief was, in fact, kind of terrifying. If Caleb didn't want him, great, but the flowers hadn't worked. He was still hungry. Starving. He wanted—well, his instincts wanted Caleb on top of him, shoving his legs apart, sating them both. Only now, he was too sick and too broken and not incubus enough to make a compelling case for that.

He was glad, and scared, and—well, he was probably going to die. That sucked.

Jasper didn't believe Poppy had meant to poison him. Sasha had called the witch her friend, and witches and demons usually got along. Or, well, if they didn't get along, he doubted any would willingly make enemies with Elrith.

"Can I see my phone?" Jasper asked.

The guy leaned over and handed it to him from a side table. Jasper pulled up the screenshot Poppy had taken.

"Is this what I ate?" He held the phone up in front of Caleb. Fuck if Jasper knew anything about the flora and fauna surrounding Lyric, but if Caleb lived out here, he probably knew.

"That's it."

Jasper frowned. "And it's always poison? To everybody? All kinds of—" He waved his hand, indicating what they were —supernatural.

"That I know of, yeah."

"Oh. Well . . . shit." There was some kind of explanation, he was sure, but he wasn't going to find it foggy headed, sick, and maybe dying.

But if he was going out, he could fill at least his stomach. He set the phone aside and dug into the soup while Caleb watched. It was kind of awkward, but Caleb nodded, satisfied, when Jasper passed it back empty.

"I'm, um . . . still hungry," Jasper admitted. He was testing things, maybe pushing too far. What would he do if Caleb grabbed him by the neck and kissed him? He didn't really want Caleb to need him the way most people did—well, he also maybe didn't want to die. Sucked that he had to hurt people or give up. Somewhere in there should've been a third option, one where he could shoot Caleb a sly smile, get what he needed, and have that be okay.

Caleb only nodded again. He moved to drop the bowl in the sink. "I need to go to the store. Pantry's sparse. I'll bring you back something. Any requests?"

Jasper chewed his lip for a second. "Do you have a phone charger?" He'd left his back at the trail's start in his Tesla.

With a jerk of his head toward the nightstand, Caleb pointed it out. "Match yours?"

"Oh, um, yeah. Great! Other than that . . . maybe a toothbrush? My mouth tastes kind of off."

Again, Caleb nodded. He didn't seem like the kind of guy who talked a lot when he didn't have to. Maybe he was out there alone a lot. It didn't seem like anyone else stayed in this cabin with him.

"And, uh, Oreos? And milk! Oreos are shit without milk."

Caleb cocked a brow at him. Okay, Oreos weren't the healthiest option, but who cared? Human food wasn't really sustenance to incubi. Jasper didn't process it the same way, could eat a pack of Oreos for breakfast every day and still be perfectly bangable. Unchanging. Devilishly attractive.

"Please? I'm having an off day."

"Oreos and milk," Caleb grumbled.

And too soon, he was grabbing his keys and leaving Jasper alone in his cabin to ponder just how entirely fucked he was.

Or wasn't.

6

CALEB

O reos.

Guy almost dies of poisoning, and he asks not for something substantive like beef or potatoes, but chocolate cookies. Apparently, Caleb's houseguest had the self-preservation instinct of a magpie.

Caleb stared at the wall of milk in the grocery store. He only ever bought the whole kind. Did a tiny guy who spent all day in the gym want the low-fat one? He looked down at the packs of cookies in his basket and shook his head.

No way. The regular full-fat kind it was. He grabbed a gallon instead of his usual half gallon and tried not to think about the plastic waste. It wasn't like he was going to buy a cow, so there wasn't much to be done about it.

He still wasn't sure what he was doing. Why hadn't he called someone to come take Jasper Jones off his hands, since he clearly needed help Caleb couldn't provide if he thought poison flowers were going to "fix" him?

Jasper Jones. He sounded like a cartoon character and looked like one of those twinky little internet models with his messy blond hair and come-hither eyes.

He'd also looked at Caleb like he wanted to eat him alive, and not in a cannibalistic kind of way.

Under that hooded gaze, all he'd been able to do was grab his keys and run out the door as fast as possible. The man had almost died. Caleb was not going to fuck him when his body was already so overtaxed.

Even if it was tempting.

He filled his cart as he wandered through the store, not in his usual efficient way, reading items from a list compiled in order of when he passed their aisles on his regular route through the store, but at random, and whatever struck his fancy.

Apparently, his fancy was a lot of carbs and not much else. He was going to get home with the ingredients to make a bread sandwich. Or a cookie one.

That seemed like an excellent plan.

He sighed and took another turn through the entire store, trying to make better choices.

More time around people, and all because his entire day had been thrown into an uproar over an adorable twink who thought he needed to be "fixed."

When he got home, Jasper was wrapped in a throw blanket from his couch, looking through a list on his TV. He hadn't realized he had such a thing on the television. Maybe he didn't, though, since in the corner it said, "Welcome, Jasper."

He looked over and glanced down at the floor. "I hope you don't mind I connected it to my account. You didn't have any logins for streaming services stored, so I used my own."

Caleb stared at him blankly for a second before shrugging. "I don't even know what you're talking about." He headed for the kitchen counter with his back to Jasper, so the man wouldn't see him blush as he admitted, "I've never actually turned the thing on. It was in the cabin when I bought it. My sister had a dish installed, but she's the one obsessed with TV."

There was a short silence, followed by a hesitant, "Did you just buy the place?"

"Ten years ago," Caleb muttered, but he didn't turn around to see if Jasper had heard.

The silence returned for a long time, so maybe he hadn't and was still waiting for an answer. Caleb turned after putting the vegetables in the crisper, to repeat himself, and almost jumped to find Jasper standing in the kitchen, blanket still wrapped around his shoulders.

"Can I help?"

Caleb grabbed a glass and the gallon of milk and set them in front of Jasper, then slid across a bag of cookies. "You can eat. You look like you're going to fall down."

Jasper gave him a sad smile but did as commanded, pouring a glass of milk and opening a bag of cookies as Caleb finished putting the groceries away.

Something about the younger man's posture, the slump of his

shoulders and hang of his head, set Caleb's teeth on edge. It was wrong. They guy was young, good looking, and obviously had money, going by his designer ripped jeans and brand new hiking boots. Nobody like that should be so unhappy.

Just as Caleb was finishing with the last bag, Jasper spoke up again. "Would you like to watch some TV with me? I guess it's not your thing, but there's this show I bet you'll like. You remind me of one of the characters."

Caleb wasn't sure why a show with a character like himself would be entertaining, but he turned to Jasper, and there was this heartbreaking kind of hope in his eyes. Like he'd asked this same question to dozens of people, and they always said no. He was expecting negative, but still, he asked.

"Sure," Caleb agreed.

Without asking if Jasper even wanted any, he made hot chocolate for both of them and thrust a mug into the man's hands as they headed for the couch. What was the point of having company if he couldn't feed them his favorite things?

He went over to snatch the heavy blanket off his bed and laid it across both of them on the couch as he sat down next to Jasper.

"I'm trusting you not to play some show about a lawyer and tell me how I'm just like him," he grumbled, and Jasper giggled and shook his head. The sweet smile looked good on him, so Caleb gave him an affected scowl and muttered, "Or a mob boss."

That earned him an outright laugh. When Jasper finished, he shook his head. "Can't think of a single one of either you remind me of, promise." He took one hand away from his two-handed grip on the hot chocolate—like he couldn't keep his hands warm, Caleb thought with a frown—and took up the remote to scroll through, finally selecting something and hitting play.

Caleb supposed the show wasn't too bad. For television. Lots of swordplay and swearing. And the lead character might have been a little . . . taciturn. It wouldn't have been the first time Caleb was compared to someone grumpy, but it was hard to deny. Also, at least this guy was good looking. He seemed to want to see the best in people, even when they let him down. Jasper was giving Caleb an awful lot of credit.

When Jasper set the remote on Caleb's lap and leaned into him, head on his shoulder, it seemed even less awful. Weird, how that kind of closeness seemed so natural to the guy.

A few episodes into the show, Jasper dozed off. Caleb pulled the empty mug from his hands and set it on the table at the end of the couch, but he didn't rouse him or push him off. It was comfortable.

He also didn't turn the television off. The show wasn't too bad, really.

7

JASPER

Caleb let Jasper sleep on him until well after the sun went down. Jasper only roused when Caleb lifted him up, the blanket still draped over him, and carried him back to bed.

If he was going to be too sleepy and loose limbed to walk to bed, this was a pretty decent alternative.

Caleb set him down gently and adjusted the blanket around his body. Groggy as he was, Jasper managed to catch his hand before he could pull away. "Stay?" he whispered. Unless Caleb was hiding an entire other half of his cabin, there was only one bed. Jasper didn't want to force him out of it.

With a scowl, Caleb considered him. "I can sleep on the couch."

If he hadn't been so dizzy, he'd have rolled his eyes. "Your bed is, like, orgy sized."

Caleb choked, turning red under his beard. "What would you know about that?"

Okay, so Jasper couldn't help rolling his eyes, even if he regretted it a second later. "Got a weird family. What I'm *saying* is that we could fit three more people in here and none of us would even have to touch. I just"—Jasper swallowed—"I don't want to kick you out of your own bed? I've already crashed your entire day. I don't have to fuck up your night too." When Caleb's scowl deepened, Jasper shrank into his shoulders. "Please?"

Caleb nodded tersely. "But I need to put wood on the fire. And change."

Jasper beamed. " 'Kay."

He watched while Caleb turned around, toward a chest of drawers. He pulled off his shirt, exposing a broad, firm back. If he hadn't seemed so standoffish, Jasper would've told him to turn around and give a little show. He was not at all used to people who didn't want him—a welcome revelation and, in this particular context, a disappointment. He didn't want Caleb to *have* to have him; he wanted Caleb to want to have him. Or show more than vague discomfort when Jasper said something racy.

He pulled on another shirt—dark and soft, without buttons— and replaced his jeans with flannel pajama pants.

"Do you have an extra pair?" Jasper sat up, suddenly keen. If he fell asleep in his skin-tight jeans, he'd regret it in the morning. "Or gym pants. Or, uh . . ."

Caleb frowned at him, but he dug around in his drawers and found a pair of gray sweatpants and a T-shirt. Jasper didn't bother getting up to kick his jeans off onto the sheepskin rug. The sweatpants were too big, but so was the T-shirt, so he tugged that over his head and left the sweatpants behind. "Perfect. Thanks."

For a second, Caleb stared at him. The shirt's short sleeves were down to Jasper's elbows. The thing practically swallowed him. Not the cutest look, but there was something soft in Caleb's expression that warmed Jasper for the first time in days.

"Okay. Fix the fire. I'm cold," Jasper pressed, earning a grumble from the grumpy bear of a man. It got him moving, though, and that meant that in moments, he'd turned off the lights and was crawling into bed, slipping under the blanket with him.

Jasper turned over. Caleb's eyes caught the firelight, but the effect wasn't the scary red glow of demon eyes. It was warm and concerned and soft.

"I didn't thank you for saving me today."

He could feel the heat rolling off of Caleb. He could've snuggled into him, but he'd already asked a lot.

All in all, this wasn't such a bad day to go out on. A big, strong, sexy man had saved his life and made him hot chocolate. Maybe Caleb didn't look at him like he just *had* to split him open, but he had watched TV with him and let him lean on his arm. He'd been kind, not because he wanted anything, but because it was his nature.

Caleb hummed. "It's fine."

Jasper nodded. He reached out slowly, and when Caleb didn't pull his hand away from where it rested on the mattress between them, Jasper set his on top of it. "Well, okay, but . . . thank you. For saving me, and for Oreos."

D<small>ESPITE</small> <small>ALL</small> <small>HIS</small> <small>BEST</small> <small>INTENTIONS</small>, by morning, Jasper had squirmed his way into the warmth of Caleb's chest to sleep under the weight of his arm, so he damn well felt it when Caleb got up.

Normally, Jasper thrived in the early morning light. He liked to go out and run, and felt like filling his days made his empty nights easier to get through.

Now, he was too tired to be bothered getting up, much less running.

Until he remembered the Oreos.

He slipped out from under Caleb's heavy blanket. Everything was fine as he walked over the sheepskin rug, but when his feet hit bare floor, he hissed. Jasper bounced the whole way to the kitchen, hopped onto a stool, and pulled his feet up, tugging Caleb's shirt down over his knees and curling it under his toes. The blisters on his feet weren't healing like they should, but they weren't so bad.

"Your shirt's in the dryer," Caleb said as he moved around the kitchen, pulling out a bowl, a whisk, and a pan.

Jasper narrowed his eyes. "Well, unless you're bringing it to me, this is what I'm wearing. I'm not walking across your ice-rink floor again." He reached for the Oreos and pulled the pack toward him. "Milk?"

Caleb sighed but poured him a glass. "You need to eat something with some substance."

Cocking a brow, Jasper shrugged. Sasha would've said that

Caleb was "something with some substance," but Jasper just pulled his lip beneath his teeth to hide a smile.

"Yes, sir."

He dipped his cookie into the milk while Caleb huffed and shuffled around and whisked eggs with grated sharp cheddar. He kept his head down, furiously beating eggs, but if Jasper didn't know better, he'd think the man'd gone a little pink around his ears.

The eggs were quick to cook, and Caleb set a bowl of them beside Jasper's pack of cookies. "Eat."

"As you wish." While Caleb watched, he lifted a forkful to his lips, took a bite, and moaned. "Delicious."

With a jerky nod, Caleb started eating his own breakfast. He leaned against the counter with his hip, one foot on top of the other. He, at least, had the wisdom to put on socks.

Jasper liked him in pajamas. Since he didn't have regular dates with people, the people he spent the night with rarely wore clothes. PJs made Caleb look warm and cozy. He could imagine sliding his hands under Caleb's shirt, feeling his stomach, the rise and fall of his breath. It'd be easy to make a game of touching everything he couldn't see while Caleb played his rumbling, scowling space heater.

"Could I—" he blurted before he thought any better of it. After a second, he cleared his throat and started again. "I parked my car at the trailhead, and I'm still feeling kind of . . . off? Would it be okay if I stayed here today? I mean, I don't want to put you out, I just . . . maybe I'm not great at the whole outdoorsy thing."

"Oh, really?" Caleb eyed Jasper's new hiking boots, set against the wall near the bed.

"Hey, shoe guy told me those were the best hiking boots he had."

"And you got them yesterday?"

Jasper grinned. "I absolutely did. For my wilderness adventure." Jasper spread his hands and moved them in an arc through the air. Just there, he saw the faintest hint of a smile on Caleb's lips. Definitely. "So, can I hang out?"

Jasper tried not to let his smile turn sour and nervous as Caleb looked him over. Finally, he shrugged. "Sure."

"Cool."

Jasper spent most of the day watching TV—some silly sitcom he didn't have to pay full attention to. Caleb didn't stay in all day, but went out and brought more wood for the stand by the fireplace. There was plenty to do out in the middle of nowhere—things Jasper hadn't ever thought about. He'd bet they didn't even have DoorDash this far out.

Meanwhile, Jasper thought he was going to *actually* starve. He couldn't eat enough. He polished off the entire pack of Oreos by himself, ate a bagel with cream cheese, toast with strawberry jam —Caleb had gone on some kind of carb binge when he'd gone to the grocery store—and ate some early spring berries from the drawer in the fridge.

At around four, Caleb finally sank into the couch beside him to watch TV, or maybe just to take a load off. For a while, Jasper didn't move much. It was nice to have company, and if he drew Caleb's attention, he'd wreck it. If Caleb didn't look at him and jump him a second later, he still might not want a lingerer. But then, Jasper's stomach growled.

Caleb stared at him. "Really?"

He'd borne witness to most of Jasper's snacking all day long.

Jasper smiled, wrinkled his nose, and shrugged. "I mean, yeah? I'm kind of hungry."

But food wasn't doing the trick; it wasn't going to. This was just his starving body telling him to take anything and everything that might make him feel full again. But he was an incubus, and no amount of cookies or carbs was going to fix what ailed him.

What if Jasper asked outright? That might fix something. Or Caleb would think he'd lost his marbles and turn him out. Shit . . . Jasper'd never had to *ask* before.

With a sigh, Caleb pushed down on his knees to get back to his feet. "I'll make you something."

Chewing his lip, Jasper looked after him. It was kind and good of Caleb to try, but it wasn't going to fix anything. It'd just be more wasted effort for Jasper's sake.

He got up from the couch to follow him. After breakfast, he'd showered and put his jeans back on, but he'd left his shirt in the dryer. It'd be fine whenever he got it, and Caleb's was comfier.

Caleb turned from the fridge and startled when he saw Jasper standing behind him. Jasper rubbed the back of his neck. "Sorry." He laughed.

"It's okay. Sandwiches?" He held up turkey and lettuce.

Jasper shook his head. "Actually, I was thinking . . ."

Shit. This was weird. Kind of a good weird though—there

was a tingle in his stomach, and he didn't know what would happen. Any second, he might fly or he might fall. There was a whole spectrum of fear and elation and hope that he had lost since he'd become a demon.

He chewed on his lip while Caleb stared down at him. Carefully, he pulled the lettuce and meat out of Caleb's hands and set them back in the fridge door. Then, he stepped in close. He gave Caleb a second to step away or to put his hands out and stop him, before he leaned up and brushed his lips across Caleb's. His beard tickled Jasper's cheeks, but his lips were soft and warm. They didn't part for him, but he didn't press in, just fell back onto his heels again.

"Maybe I'm hungry for something else," Jasper suggested. "If it's okay, I could . . . stay the night? Like, actually stay the night." His hands shook a little, so he set his palms flat against Caleb's chest.

All Caleb was doing was staring down at him like he'd gone crazy, and Jasper fought the urge to sink into his shoulders. Demonic incubus magnetism or not, he was *still* an incubus— still attractive, vaguely functional, even. Hell, he was a pretty decent lay on his own merit.

He liked that if Caleb didn't want him, he could say no—he really did. But if Jasper said what he wanted out loud and Caleb rebuffed him, he thought he might shatter.

"If you want," Jasper continued into the silence, his lips a nervous tremble of a smile. "I do. Want. Uh, you? If that's okay?"

Jasper's right hand slid up to cup Caleb's neck, and when he tried to pull him down for another kiss, Caleb let him.

8

CALEB

Caleb had never been asked such a thing before, so simply, like there was no art required, no artifice. Relationships, or even one-night-stands, had required special clothes, loud clubs, dancing, and a dozen other things Caleb either hated or was terrible at.

They had never been as simple as "do you want a sandwich?"—"No, thanks, I'd rather have you."

But there it was; there Jasper was, asking it exactly like that.

It was perfect.

He wrapped his arms around Jasper's slim waist and kissed him back. When Jasper lifted one long leg to wrap around his hips, he forewent a dozen in between steps and grabbed the man's ass, hoisting him up and letting him wrap the other leg around him. He hardly weighed more than a few sacks of the previous day's groceries, he was so small.

Caleb nudged the fridge closed with his foot and walked them over to the bed.

Oh damn, did he have lube? Condoms? They were both supernaturals, so it wasn't likely any diseases were communicable, but one never knew. Plus it was just good manners to offer.

He pulled back the blanket and lay Jasper across the bed, then reached for the drawer on the bedside table. Lube, he had. He was a fan of lube. Condoms, he hadn't really needed in the cabin. On the odd occasion he'd gone into the city and danced the ridiculous mating dance, he hadn't brought anyone home with him; he'd always gone to their place and slipped out before dawn.

After a moment of frantic searching, Jasper's hand grabbed his. "Don't worry about that. It's fine." He took the lube, opened it, took a long look down Caleb's body, and squirted a liberal amount of the stuff onto his fingers. Caleb knew a compliment when he saw one, and couldn't help the smile that played across his lips.

"Worried?"

"Not even a little," Jasper answered, no hesitation in his voice. "Can't wait."

Again, no artifice. No games. Who was Jasper Jones, and how the hell was he so perfect?

Caleb made short work of Jasper's clothes, even those painted-on jeans, and then undressed himself more slowly, watching as Jasper worked himself open on his own fingers.

"Gonna wreck me?" he whispered, eyes shining with anticipation in the firelight.

When Caleb dropped his flannel pants to the floor, freeing his cock, Jasper immediately reached for it, spreading the rest of the lube onto the head before running his whole hand down Caleb's cock. He wrapped his fingers around it, testing the weight and girth, and apparently liking what he found.

"That what you want?" Caleb tossed his shirt to the rug and met Jasper's eyes again. "Want me to split you open and leave you ruined for anyone else?"

He relaxed back onto the pillows and looked up at Caleb coyly. "That's exactly what I want."

When Caleb climbed between his legs, Jasper automatically wound them around his back, pulling him forward. Caleb leaned down and nipped his full lower lip. "Gotta give me a second to get inside you. Not gonna hurt you."

"You won't," Jasper insisted, pushing his hips up impatiently.

Still, Caleb pushed in slow and steady, and everything about it was perfect. Jasper was as ready as he insisted, and he opened beautifully, all soft hitching breaths and a tiny pleased smile when Caleb bottomed out inside him.

He let out all the air in his lungs and leaned down to rest their foreheads together.

"So perfect," Jasper whispered against his lips. "Perfect cock, perfect body, perfect gentleman. How's a guy get so perfect?"

Caleb pulled out and slid back in, just as slowly, without moving away from Jasper. "Can't say anybody's ever called me that before. Maybe a guy has to rise to the occasion when he finds someone this sweet."

Jasper grinned at him, reaching up to cup his cheeks and kissing him breathless again. "Now fuck me."

Caleb couldn't imagine not obliging. He reached up to twine their hands together, pressing Jasper into the mattress as he pulled out again.

This time he didn't slow down.

He slammed his hips forward, spearing Jasper on his cock, and was rewarded with a punched-out moan and a "yes, fuck, just like that." Jasper's words turned into an incoherent mash of yeses and pleases as Caleb sped the rhythm of his hips, pushing his cock all the way in with every thrust, balls slapping against that pert little ass.

The heat built in his groin, and his world narrowed to that one point, his cock sliding into Jasper's tight, perfect, inviting heat, and he thrust so hard the bed squeaked against the wooden floor.

Jasper arched up in ecstasy, moaning Caleb's name as he came across his own belly without even being touched; the friction of them fucking enough to set him off.

His ass squeezed Caleb so tight, spasming around him, and pulled him over the edge too, fireworks behind his closed eyelids and white-hot electricity surging through him. He leaned down and bit Jasper's neck as he came inside him, and Jasper let out another ecstatic moan, clearly approving of the bite.

They lay there like that for a few moments, panting and coming down from the high of release, before Caleb even took his mouth off Jasper's neck. He'd left the red impression of his teeth there, but it was already fading, so no actual damage done.

When he pulled back and looked at Jasper, his eyes were half closed and glazed over, a dazed smile on his lips. "Best ever," he muttered.

Caleb had a hard time believing that, except . . . well, he wasn't sure he'd ever had sex that good before. He was usually worried about breaking his partner the whole time, and despite Jasper's slightness, for some reason, it hadn't even crossed his mind.

The man had survived serious poisoning—he was clearly pretty sturdy. On the other hand, he had *just* survived serious poisoning, and Caleb probably wasn't helping anything by taxing his body like that.

He pulled out, and Jasper hissed in displeasure but fell back against the bed, still looking debauched and entirely sated, sweaty and panting. It made a damn pretty picture. Caleb could get used to a beautiful, naked, exhausted Jasper in his bed.

Hell, who couldn't?

Caleb leaned down and kissed Jasper's sweaty brow, and headed for the bathroom to grab a wet washrag to clean them both up. When he finished, he lay down next to Jasper, and for the first time since they started kissing, he felt awkward.

Was that all Jasper had wanted?

Or, oh hells, had Jasper only offered because he felt guilty for Caleb saving him? Was it some kind of repayment for his help? He hated to imagine the nicest thing that had happened to him in years had been nothing more than a one-time "thanks for not letting me die."

If it had been, he was struck by the unhealthy urge to follow

Jasper around and save his life as often as possible. If that was all it was to him, though—

Jasper rolled over, throwing an arm across his chest, looking up at Caleb with a small smile on his face. "It was really me."

"What was you?"

"You wanted me. Wanted that." A tiny hint of doubt entered his face, drawing his brows together. "Right?"

"Yeah," Caleb agreed, reaching out to smooth that troubled brow with his fingertips. "I'd take it instead of a sandwich any day. Every day."

Jasper smiled dreamily, closing his eyes and cradling his head on Caleb's shoulder. "That would be amazing. I'd like that." And before Caleb could even ask if he was serious, if he meant that he was interested in more than one night while he was still recovering, Jasper was asleep.

Poor guy was still recovering from being poisoned, so Caleb didn't jostle him, just let him sleep. He needed it more than Caleb needed his arm free.

9

JASPER

When Jasper woke in the morning, it was to faint sunlight falling over Caleb's face, bringing out the copper in his dark beard, the smoothness of his cheeks. His lips were pink and soft, and Jasper licked his own, remembering the taste of them.

But he didn't wake because he was feeling better. He hadn't felt the usual pull of energy when Caleb came. Hell, Jasper normally needed that to get over the edge himself, but with Caleb holding his hands, close enough that the hair on his chest tickled Jasper's and their breaths mingled, all he'd needed was Caleb.

It was perfect, and Jasper wished he could've had it again and again forever.

If he couldn't eat, though, he couldn't keep Caleb. He supposed that was the trade-off, and it'd been worth it to know that, for one night, Caleb really wanted him. It'd been about the both of them. Caleb hadn't wanted to hurt him, and Jasper hadn't tried to take too much. It hadn't been a mindless fury; Caleb had put his forehead on Jasper's and kissed him. After, he hadn't passed out, exhausted from fucking and Jasper's feeding. He'd held him against his chest.

Jasper felt his smile began to tremble. He'd wanted that so much, and he got it, and now? He wasn't sure. Couldn't think about it. The demonic part of him that needed Caleb's energy was too empty or broken or weak to take it. And maybe that was okay.

Caleb had said every day—Jasper could give him all the days he had.

His throat had gotten tight while he watched Caleb's eyelids flutter softly in sleep, and thought about how much he wanted those days to last. Quietly, he got out of bed and pulled on Caleb's big shirt. He needed to do something more than sit there and be sad.

Caleb had spent the last couple days taking care of him. This time, Jasper would make breakfast for Caleb instead.

In the kitchen, he tried to stay quiet. He didn't eat a lot of human food, so he wasn't a very good cook, but he'd watched Caleb make eggs, and that seemed easy enough—crack them, whisk them up with some salt and pepper and milk and maybe some cheese, then cook them in a pan. He could manage that.

He cracked half a dozen eggs into a bowl and turned on the stovetop so the pan could heat up. He put a pat of butter in it before he moved to season and whisk the eggs.

Something about the spin of broken yolks or the way the heat from the stovetop hit him in the face when he turned around made Jasper sway. Before he knew what was happening, he stumbled.

The bowl clattered on the stovetop, splashing raw egg across the heating plate to seep under the pan and drip down the front of the oven. Jasper had barely had time to catch himself on the oven's handle before he sagged against it, the smell of burning egg and cheese right under his nose.

Slowly, he lowered himself to the kitchen floor. "Shit," he whispered, bracing his forehead on the oven's cool steel front, vaguely aware of Caleb calling his name as he scrambled out of bed.

Then, Caleb was right there. He flicked off the burner and knelt in front of Jasper, still clinging to the oven door.

When he grabbed Jasper's face, Jasper finally let go.

"Are you okay?" Caleb demanded. His rough-skinned thumbs brushed his cheeks, his pretty eyes swam with concern.

Jasper smiled sadly and nodded.

With furrowed brow, Caleb remained unconvinced. His hand pressed Caleb's forehead. "You're freezing."

That was it, wasn't it? Incubi who couldn't feed turned all that hunger inward, taking it from their own bodies until their blood stopped pumping.

"It's okay," Jasper whispered. Last night, Caleb had given him exactly what he'd always wanted. Lots of people never got that much. "I'm so sorry I made a mess." His gaze wandered to a drip of yellow down the oven's front, and Jasper grimaced. "I wanted to cook you breakfast."

Caleb shook his head. "That doesn't matter. Here—" He scooped Jasper up in his arms and carried him over to the couch. He set him there, nestled in the corner between the back and the arm rest, lifted his feet to tuck in against the cushions, and wrapped a soft blanket around him.

Then he sat on the coffee table and leaned toward Jasper, reaching out to set a hand on his knee. "Is this—was last night too much?"

Jasper couldn't help laughing, which only deepened Caleb's frown. He couldn't have that, so he reached for Caleb's hand and slipped their fingers together. "No. It's not that. Last night was really, really, *really* perfect, Caleb. The best. This doesn't have anything to do with you."

He wished Caleb would smile for him. He looked so damned concerned. If he knew Jasper was a demon who wanted to feed on him, maybe he wouldn't bother caring.

"Will you please tell me what's going on?" Caleb asked, turning his hand so he could rub his thumb over Jasper's knuckles.

Jasper swallowed. It might be kinder to tell Caleb the truth and set him free of this whole mess. Or maybe, Caleb, sweet as he was, would feel even more responsible. But he didn't have a magic dick—a *fantastic* dick, yes, but not a magic one. The problem was Jasper's.

"If there were anything you could do, I would tell you," Jasper whispered, his voice catching on renewed tightness in his throat.

Caleb looked ready to argue with him, so Jasper shook his head. He forced a smile. "I'll be fine," he lied. "I'm just hungry."

That, Caleb could fix. He nodded, rising immediately. "I'll make you something."

"Actually"—Caleb froze and looked back at him, ready to do whatever it took. It broke Jasper's heart that it wouldn't matter. "That hot chocolate you made me the first night? It was really good. Could I have that?" Caleb looked pained, but something about the warm, rich brew reminded him of the man. "Please?"

With a jerky nod, Caleb said, "Okay, but you're going to eat some real food too."

"Deal."

And before Caleb pressed a plate of bacon and eggs and more toast than any one man could eat on him, he handed off a mug of hot chocolate that Jasper cradled to his chest.

10

CALEB

Jasper wasn't getting better.

Oh, he was better in that he wasn't dead of poison, but as time passed the dizzy spells got worse, and they were joined by a listless boredom.

Once, Caleb looked up to find Jasper looking at him like a starving man looked at a steak. He'd immediately thought of taking the man to bed and giving him a sound fucking, but Jasper was clearly ill, and sex was not going to help that.

Jasper had to be a supernatural to have survived the flowers, and Caleb was starting to mentally catalogue the kinds who ate people. There weren't many, and barring vampires, none were so beautiful. Jasper had spent enough time in the sun, and he seemed far less intent on Caleb's major arteries than other major parts of him.

Caleb fed him and fed him, until most people would have

popped. Until Jasper clutched his stomach and groaned, mumbling something about Caleb fattening him up to eat him.

It didn't help. He gave him another dose of the remedy for the damned flowers, and Jasper made a face at the flavor of it, but it didn't do much either.

Nothing helped.

One night, after almost a week of "I'll just stay one more day"s, they were curled up on the couch, watching some mindless comedy show, when Jasper looked up at him, eyes unfocused and half closed. "Can we go out and look at the stars?"

Maybe some men could have said no to that, but Caleb was not one of them. He was weak, okay?

So he wrapped Jasper in the blanket from his bed and carried him up to the cabin's loft, through the window, and out onto the roof. He laid down next to him, and Jasper moved to cover him up, so they were both draped in blanket.

"It's beautiful," Jasper whispered after a while.

Caleb didn't want to admit he'd never paid much attention. He was a land-bound kind of guy, and the stars were just something that existed. They weren't important to him. Or, well, they hadn't been. He brushed Jasper's hair back from his face and kissed his cheek. "It is," he agreed.

"I wish we could stay here like this forever," Jasper whispered as he snuggled into the space under Caleb's arm. He fit there perfectly, like Caleb had been carved just to hold him. "It's hard to see the stars from Lyric. This is much better."

"It is better." Caleb wasn't sure whether he meant that the cabin was better than Lyric, or something else.

No, that wasn't true. He knew. The cabin was better than life in the city, but life in the cabin had gotten so much better since he'd stumbled over Jasper.

He'd been well aware of the hole in his life, and not just because of Poppy's prodding, but he hadn't had any idea how to fix it. It had seemed like an insurmountable obstacle. Caleb didn't like to leave his cabin, but he also wanted to find someone to be in the cabin with him.

In his dreams, he couldn't have imagined anyone better than soft, sweet Jasper.

If only soft, sweet Jasper didn't have some horrible mystery illness that was making him weaker and weaker by the day, Caleb could have someone to spend his days and his nights with. Someone to lie with him by the fire and drink cocoa all winter.

"Thank you," Jasper whispered. "Thank you for everything."

The words made Caleb want to curl in on himself. It didn't sound like thank you. It sounded like goodbye.

He wanted to answer, if only to talk to Jasper more, but what could he say? He hadn't given the man anything but a place to stay while he recovered from the poison. And of course, he wasn't recovering. He was getting worse as time went on, and nothing Caleb did made a difference.

The moment Caleb voiced that, he felt like something would break. Maybe something between them, maybe something inside himself, but something irreparable. So instead, he pulled Jasper tighter against him and leaned down to kiss him on the top of the head.

All he could do for the time being, while Jasper refused to tell him what was wrong, was keep hoping he would get better.

A few moments later, Jasper gave a soft snore from his place on Caleb's shoulder. He should move them inside. Jasper would be more comfortable indoors, with the fire.

He looked up at the stars for a long time, wishing on each one he could see for a way to fix whatever was wrong, so Jasper could stay.

If he wanted to.

11

JASPER

He wasn't getting better. He wasn't going to get better. And watching Caleb come to terms with that, realizing he cared, was awful.

Jasper could've told him what was wrong, but what would that fix? Saying he couldn't feed off Caleb would make it seem like that was what he'd wanted all along, right? Like he'd just asked Caleb to bed so he could recover and move on. And it wouldn't change the fact that he couldn't feed off him. That was a problem somewhere inside Jasper, not another shitty inconvenience to put on Caleb's plate.

He'd never told a human what he was. He'd seen the lust in their eyes, let it play out, but humans remained largely ignorant of the supernatural. They were far from the only creatures on the planet though. And none who knew about incubi particularly liked them. If Caleb didn't hate him on principle, knowing what he was would reframe their whole time together, every kiss and smile and soft touch. He wanted to leave them as they were in Caleb's memory—the way he actually meant them.

After how kind Caleb had been, it wasn't that Jasper was certain he'd hate him, but he wasn't ready for the easy dismissal —the assumption that Caleb finally knew what Jasper was about. He was a demon, and a leeching one at that.

Much to his father's disappointment, he wasn't even any good at it.

Jasper was curled up on the couch again. Caleb had set the remote on the arm of the couch near his head, but it was an awful lot of effort to twist around, grab it, and commit to watching something on the TV.

His eyes stung. He wanted to cry. He hadn't been sick since he'd hit puberty and demoned out, but when he was a kid, he'd had the flu a few times. Always, at some point, he'd get so fucking sick of being sick he'd melt into a puddle of tears.

This was worse, because he had a feeling that when he stopped being sick, that was it.

At the edge of his consciousness, he heard an annoying buzz, but it wasn't until Caleb walked to the bedside table, frowned down at it, and brought him his phone that he remembered it existed at all.

Out in the woods, he'd been without signal for days. And, well, he felt like shit and hadn't wanted to talk to anybody. It was hard to make friends when you got everyone all hot and bothered. His family weren't the sorts of people you wanted to expose your vulnerabilities to, generally speaking, and Jasper was already the weak link there.

"I think someone's trying to get in contact with you," Caleb said as he approached the couch, Jasper's phone in his outstretched hand.

Jasper lifted his head, blinking some of the stinging tears from his eyes. He smiled. "Thanks."

All the text messages he'd gotten in the last few days hit one after the other.

Sasha: *Did it work?*

Sasha: *Helloooo???*

Sasha: *I went to see Poppy. She said you'd be fine. Are you fine?*

He was pretty decidedly not fine, but it didn't sound like Poppy'd pointed him the wrong way on purpose . With a flick of his thumb, he scrolled on.

Sasha: *Jasper.*

Sasha: *Jasper, you can't just disappear on me forever.*

Sasha: *Jasper, are you okay??*

Sasha: *Listen, I know things are fucked up. This isn't really . . . for you. I get it. But you're my brother, and I need to know you're okay. If you need to disappear, fine, but can you just let me know you're okay first?*

Sasha: *. . . I really hope it worked.*

Malcolm: *Dad wants us all over for dinner tonight. Text me.*

The last, Jasper could ignore. Elrith wouldn't want anything to do with an incubus who couldn't even keep himself standing. But he owed more to Sasha than that.

Shifting in his seat to free up both hands, he typed her a quick message.

I'm fine. Promise. I met someone. Tell you all about it soon. I love you.

He sent the message off and tucked his phone between the couch cushion and the arm of the seat like that'd block out the signal again. He liked things better when the outside world didn't try and creep in. He didn't want to think about what else he'd leave behind if he didn't recover.

"Everything all right?" Caleb asked.

It was obvious he wanted to press for more, but he caught himself. Already, Jasper was holding him too far away. Maybe he couldn't tell Caleb what he wanted to know, but he could tell him some stuff. If Caleb could see him as a person, that'd be wonderful.

"Yeah. Just . . . family stuff. Do you have a sister?"

Caleb grunted. After a long moment, he shrugged then nodded. "Yeah."

"Mine worries. Her name's Sasha. Um, we have the same dad? Different moms though. She was, uh, already living with Dad when I met him the first time." Even though he and Sasha were roughly the same age, girls hit puberty sooner. It seemed like a rough deal, really. Being an incubus sucked enough a few years closer to adulthood. Jasper had always been glad he was a boy, if only because it meant having a normal life that much longer. He wished he'd known what was coming, though, so he could have enjoyed that time more. "She was just checking up on me. I guess I kind of dropped off the radar?"

Jasper chewed his lip for a second, then dropped his cheek on his knee and turned his head so he could keep looking at

Caleb without having to hold it up. "But this . . ." He waved at himself. "Getting sick—it's not really part of the McKittack family creed."

Caleb crossed his arms, but the annoyance that furrowed his brow wasn't directed at Jasper. "People get sick. That's not your fault. Your family wouldn't stand beside you through it?"

"Sasha, maybe, but I think they'd mostly blame me for it." Caleb looked like he wanted to hit someone. Best if they moved on. "You're a shifter?"

Caleb nodded. "Bear."

Jasper chuckled. "That makes complete sense." When he turned, no doubt Caleb would be enormous and fluffy and wonderful. It'd be so cool to run his fingers through Caleb's fur. "Were you always able to turn?"

Caleb shook his head. He perched on the coffee table, so Jasper didn't have to turn his head quite as much to meet his eyes.

"Me either," Jasper admitted. "I mean, I don't shift that much. I just . . . wasn't always, uh, what I am. And we're supposed to, like, rally to it. Paranormal pride and all that. But I don't think —" Jasper swallowed hard. "I don't think what I am, what we are, is good."

It was the first time he'd admitted it out loud, despite how the worry had bounced around in his head for years. His eyes started to sting again, but then there was a broad, warm hand pressed flat against his cheek. Caleb didn't hesitate to comfort him for a single second.

"I do," Caleb said, deep voice so soft it matched Jasper's

broken whisper. "What we are isn't who we are. You are good, Jasper Jones."

Jasper's bottom lip trembled, so he bit it. A moment later, when a tear streaked down from the corner of his eye over the bridge of his nose and toward his knee, Caleb caught it on a fingertip and brushed it away.

"You too, Caleb."

12

CALEB

They were reaching an end, and they both knew it. Jasper barely had the strength to stand up and move himself between the bed and the couch, so he was staying in bed. It wasn't like he paid any attention when he had the television anymore.

Caleb looked longingly back at the days, a whole week ago, when Jasper would smile and engage with the shows they watched, pointing out how hot an actor was, or how annoying a character. Sometimes even mouthing the lines out at the same time as the characters on screen.

Caleb had called Poppy a dozen times, but she wasn't answering. He'd even driven into the city, to her shop, to try to get her to help. Despite the fact that it had been the middle of her business hours, the door had been locked and the shop dark.

He'd have broken in, but a police car had driven by, and that didn't seem like the best answer anyway.

If Poppy didn't want to be found, there was usually a reason. Probably an annoying one, but she didn't disappear on him often. He'd gone home annoyed.

He sat there just after twilight, watching Jasper sleep fitfully, eating his turkey sandwich. Turkey sandwiches weren't the food of the gods at their very best, but this one tasted like sawdust in his mouth. His throat was so dry he could barely force it down, swallowing repeatedly and reaching for his water to try to clear it from his throat.

" 'M sorry," Jasper moaned in his sleep. "Didn't mean to."

Caleb took the excuse to drop the remains of the sandwich back on his plate and head over to check on Jasper. He sat on the edge of the bed and carded his hand through the man's hair, sweat damp as it was. "You don't need to be sorry."

Jasper shook his head almost violently, and for a second, Caleb thought he'd woken. Then he settled, eyes still closed, and mumbled, "Just wanted someone to want me, not the demon."

Demon? There was no way sweet little Jasper was a demon. Well, except he'd practically told Caleb he was.

I don't think what I am, what we are, is good.

Somehow, even as the notion penetrated his admittedly thick skull, it didn't change anything. So Jasper was a demon. Caleb wasn't a proper werebear like he'd implied either, was he? No, he was half fae, and the bear part had come later. Lots of people hated fae as much as they hated demons, and for good reason.

There weren't a lot of things that made demons sick, though, and Jasper's problem kept circling back to starvation. He was

POISONWOOD   67

starving to death because he wouldn't—couldn't?—eat what he needed to.

Caleb pulled out his phone and dialed Poppy.

Again, no answer.

He sighed and scowled at the phone. He had an annoying feeling that the moment he figured this out, his irritating sister would be right back to banging on his door, demanding that he watch movies and do other things normal people did.

If Jasper were alive when it happened, he'd agree to it.

He heard Poppy's voice in his head then, as clear as if she'd been standing right next to him.

"It's a corrupted forest spirit, gone feral and violent."

The story came flooding back to him in a rush. Poppy had told him about the Poisonwood monster back when he'd moved into the cabin. She'd wanted him to rethink moving into the woods by himself, and so, compared him to a corrupted nature spirit.

The Poisonwood monster was a tale about a spirit that had broken away from its purpose—protecting the forest—and hidden itself away, attacking everyone who came near.

The story had been intended to scare children out of the forest.

It had been intended to make him see that hiding from the world wasn't healthy.

It also said that eating the heart of the monster could cure any ailment. That should include starvation, shouldn't it? And even if it weren't a permanent cure, it would give them more time to figure this out. There had to be a way for Jasper to eat whatever it was he needed without hurting anyone.

He thought back to the way Jasper had looked at him a few times, with hunger in his eyes. It could have been plain old lust. It could have been—

Caleb stopped and looked down at where Jasper tossed and turned. Beautiful in every way. Perfect body. Angelic face.

He almost groaned with realization. Of course he was an incubus. And his sweet Jasper was worried about hurting people.

That was it, then. All he had to do was find the Poisonwood monster, kill it, and feed Jasper its heart. Easy peasy.

He leaned down and kissed Jasper on the forehead. "I've got to go out, but I'll be back soon." He was sure Jasper didn't hear him, but saying it seemed the sensible thing anyway.

It was a simple task, but Caleb wasn't unintelligent. He knew it wasn't an easy one. He wasn't sure that Jasper would wake up and be coherent again without help, but he needed to leave a note anyway, just in case.

> *Gone to find the Poisonwood monster. I'll be back if I can.*
> *Love, Caleb*

It was strange, seeing the word "love" there, in his own hand-writing. He'd only known Jasper a short time, but he didn't feel like he couldn't say it to him. Or maybe the note was for Poppy, since Jasper would probably die if Caleb did. He loved her too, so that was fine. If he failed, at least she wouldn't have to wonder what had happened to him.

He headed out in human form, since it was most comfortable for him, and he knew right where he was going. He'd always made a point of avoiding that part of the woods.

In the stories, the creature of legend was always hard to find. The Poisonwood monster was no white stag or golden fish. It was, like Caleb, a bear. A huge, angry, ancient bear.

As though it felt him enter its territory, he heard a roar the moment he stepped into the clearing near its cave. This entire part of the woods felt different. Not dark and foreboding, but somehow wilder. Not like they were far from the city, but like there was no city left anywhere.

Caleb barely had time to push off his boots and unbutton his jeans before the monster came rushing out of its cave, roaring again in challenge. He had expected to have to spend more time searching, at least—but no, this was better. Time was of the essence, after all.

He forced down his jeans and threw himself into the shift, pushing toward the monster. It was bigger than he was. Angrier too, which was something he wouldn't have thought possible. Poppy probably would have made a joke about it.

Still, the monster didn't need to win like Caleb did. Maybe the odds weren't in his favor, but Jasper needed this, needed Caleb to do this for him. The monster didn't have Jasper waiting at home.

It threw itself at him with reckless abandon, ignoring Caleb's claws, and raked its own across his chest. His blood, hot and bright, sprayed across his face. All he could see was red.

This creature was what stood between him and Jasper getting

well. This creature had long outlived its time, and Jasper was still so young. This creature was nothing nature had intended, and its death could give Caleb a chance at happiness.

It lunged at him. He fell to one side, ducking the worst of its claws, but it still managed to clip him on the shoulder.

He lunged from the side, going for the monster's throat. A longer fight gave the monster the advantage. Caleb had to end this as quickly as possible.

It roared and swiped at him with its claws, hitting the already open wounds on his chest. Caleb roared in pain, losing his grip on the creature, which rolled away. It didn't stay gone long, scrambling onto its feet and launching itself at Caleb again.

And again.

Caleb could feel himself weakening with every drop of blood he lost, but he couldn't stop. He couldn't.

He had to think like a man, not a bear.

He fell back, pretended to fall onto his side, slowed his breathing, and listened. When the monster came to have a look at him, probably claw his throat open and make sure he was dead, he lunged up and clawed its throat out.

The world went wobbly around him as he struck, though, and when he landed on top of the bleeding creature, he found that he couldn't get back up. Couldn't move at all.

Dammit, was all he could think as the world around him went dark, and then disappeared entirely.

13

JASPER

Even when Jasper had stopped getting out of bed, had stopped paying attention to the rising and setting of the sun, he could mark the passage of time when, every night, Caleb crawled into bed. He'd shift into the center of the mattress and wrap his strong arm around Jasper's middle. His breath would tickle as he buried his nose against Jasper's skin.

It was nice not to be alone, to have someone hold him just because they wanted to. Jasper couldn't imagine ever wanting to find the end of Caleb, that point where he'd be ready for him to leave. Of course, the reason he had this much time with Caleb to start was that there was going to be an end.

That night, Caleb didn't come to bed. When it got late, Jasper whined into the pillow, but Caleb didn't come. Too unwell to rouse, Jasper didn't get up, hardly opened his eyes.

It wasn't until morning, when the sunlight fell over the empty half of the bed, that Jasper registered Caleb wasn't there.

For a second, he worried this had all been too much. He was a stranger. He'd poisoned himself, wound up on Caleb's couch, and then demanded his care and attention for days while he got worse and worse. Of course Caleb wouldn't want to be there—what was more startling was that he'd left instead of kicking Jasper out.

Through one shaking breath, then another, Jasper allowed himself to feel miserable. But that was only because he was predisposed to it. When he chewed his lip, he realized that there wasn't one time, not one, that Caleb had been anything but kind to him. Jasper could've puked in his boots, stolen every thick and warm blanket in the whole place for himself, and told Caleb he had no taste in hot chocolate—a blatant lie, of course—and he still didn't think Caleb would abandon him. He'd be a grump, sure, but nothing about Caleb seemed like the kind of man who'd leave Jasper in a lurch.

Mustering what was left of his strength, Jasper pulled himself out of bed. Every part of him felt heavy. He ached from not moving, and his blood pumped too slow. It was hard to get enough air with each breath.

But he saw the note on the table and shuffled over to it. Once he read it, he bit his lip. Jasper had never been a big fan of "monsters." There was not a single justifiable reason for Caleb to go hunting one down.

The sign off was—was sweet. Was it meant for Jasper? Caleb hadn't had any other visitors in the week Jasper had been there, so maybe. Love—hell, what a far-off dream that'd become.

Whatever Caleb meant, it didn't really matter when he said

he was going after a monster with too little confidence about whether or not he'd come back.

Clumsily, Jasper shoved his legs into his jeans one at a time, stuffed his feet into socks and then into his new boots. As an afterthought, he grabbed one of Caleb's coats and shrugged it on. It draped heavy on Jasper's shoulders, warm and safe. It was still morning, dewy and cold, and Jasper was already freezing.

"Caleb," he shouted when he got outside. A few birds twittered and flew off, but there was no other response. "Caleb!"

He took a few steps, not knowing where he was headed. He wasn't a hiker and wasn't familiar with Poisonwood, but—as much as he sometimes felt it—he wasn't useless, either.

Jasper closed his eyes, focusing on Caleb's scent. He was all chocolate and beard oil and smoke. Sweet and good and—and everything Jasper wanted. If nothing else, Jasper was a predator, and he could hunt down his preferred prey—burly men with kind eyes and rough hands.

On will alone, he forced one foot after another until he was in a dark part of the forest. Caleb had to be okay, or Jasper was never going to find his way back.

Well, what did that matter? If Caleb wasn't coming with him, there was no point in going back to his cabin to wait out the last beats of his faltering heart.

When he found Caleb, the first thing he saw was simply an enormous brown mountain of fur.

It took him a moment to realize it wasn't one bear, but two, one collapsed on top of the other. From there, all he saw was

Caleb. His brown bear, atop what had to have been the monster he'd written about.

"Caleb!" Jasper rushed to him. He grunted as he pulled him over. Caleb rolled off the creature and onto the forest floor. His eyes fluttered open for a second, at first huge and dark, but then, starting with those eyes and rippling through his whole body, Caleb shifted into his human form in the space of a few heartbeats; no longer than it took him to hit the ground. Jasper scrambled after him, but his eyes were once again closed.

There, down his bare chest, were enormous claw marks that ripped long red gashes into Caleb's tan skin. Blood matted his chest hair down, and he didn't rouse.

Jasper pressed his hand to the wounds, like he could knit them back together. Caleb groaned. He was breathing. How hardy were shifters? Fuck.

"Caleb? Are you . . ." Of course he wasn't okay! He was torn to shreds, and they were stuck out here in the middle of nowhere with a dead monster. Why the actual fucking fuck had Caleb gone after a monster? "What can I do?"

That seemed to rouse something in Caleb. His eyes twitched and fluttered open. "Eat it."

"What?" Jasper blinked. Caleb was hardly the first person to snap those words at him, but Jasper didn't think he meant it in the regular incubus way.

"The heart," Caleb rasped. "You've gotta eat the heart."

Jasper grimaced. He looked at the creature he'd pulled Caleb off of. It was an enormous bear. In fact, it looked a lot like Caleb had when he'd been shifted, but larger, and with a heavy scowl and jagged razor-sharp teeth.

He knew it was a hunter thing, to eat the heart of your first kill, but it'd always kind of freaked him out. There were demons who bought into that kind of practice. Hell, he could just see Malcolm licking blood off his pale fingertips to impress Elrith.

"I—I can't do that, Caleb. We need to get you home. I need—" He looked over Caleb's body. Naked and enormous, it'd be a task just to get him in clothes. Jasper couldn't very well carry him back to the cabin.

But Caleb's hand lashed out startlingly fast. He gripped Jasper's arm and pulled himself up, his eyes wide and manic. "I know what you are."

Fuck. Fuck, fuck, fuck.

Jasper stared until his eyes felt dry and tight. He could fold in on himself, shrink until there was nothing left. Caleb was staring too intently. His grip was too tight. Jasper's slow heart ached.

But Caleb pulled him in. His thumb brushed Jasper's arm in a firm, soothing stroke. "It's okay. You have to eat the heart. It'll fix —everything."

Biting both lips between his teeth so they pressed into a thin line, Jasper stared at the monster of a bear. Its throat was torn in a gaping, gory half-moon. "But—"

"It's okay," Caleb promised.

"I don't want to die," Jasper whispered. He needed Caleb to know that—needed to excuse that he was even considering doing what Caleb asked.

"You won't."

"You'll come home?" With his hand already bloody, he touched Caleb's neck. His pulse beat steadily under Jasper's palm.

Caleb's smile trembled, but he inclined his head in a short nod.

"Okay. Okay."

Jasper could do this. If it meant he might not lose his sweet, crazy bear, he'd try. And Caleb had promised to come home with him. With his hands already slick with blood, what did it matter if Jasper got messier?

He backed away. The taste of his tongue soured, so he glanced at his bear. Again, Caleb nodded encouragingly.

Jasper wished he could turn away, hide, but there was nowhere to go. He couldn't just reach blunt, human fingers into a monster's chest and rip out his heart. This was demon business, and Caleb would see all of it.

He ducked his head as he let that side of him out. Small, black horns curled out from the backs of his temples, framing his light hair. His eyes shone red. His canines sharpened. Claws grew from his nail beds.

He thought to shrug out of Caleb's jacket, but it was too late —Caleb's blood was already on it. If they got through this, he'd front the dry-cleaning bill.

Jasper knelt on the other side of the monster. Briefly, he caught Caleb's eye and looked away at once. He could do this; he just couldn't watch Caleb see it all.

"It's okay," Caleb repeated.

It very much wasn't, but if this was the thing that Jasper had to do to get Caleb home, if there were even a chance that it'd help, he would try.

Digging a heart out of a bear's ribcage was pretty much the worst thing he'd done in his life. Inside, the monster's chest was still warm. Wet.

Jasper lifted the enormous organ to his parted lips. Thank god for sharp demon teeth that tore shredded muscle. He chewed and swallowed, bite after bite, as quickly as he could.

He could feel Caleb watching, but he couldn't stand to look at him. Not while he looked like this. Not while he was eating a creature's raw heart.

When he was done, his hands were slick and bloody. He wiped them off on his jeans, but his fingers were stained. It dried thick around his claws, and Jasper's lips trembled. He was full, and he was horrified.

"I'm so sorry," he whispered, hanging his head, unsure if he was speaking to Caleb or to the monster or to the whole damn world.

On unsteady legs, he rose. But things were easier once he'd freed his demon side. He rolled his shoulders back, a small measure of his strength returning just because he was now something with horns and claws and scary teeth.

"Let's get you home," Jasper said. He passed Caleb his jeans and boots. With claws, he wasn't much use helping him put them on, but he held out Caleb's coat too. "If you lean on me, do you think you can walk?"

For the first time since the whole bloody mess had started, he looked up at Caleb and found the man staring at him dreamily.

Or possibly staring through him. He must have lost a lot of blood to the bear, damn him. But also, there was the chance his memories of this would be hazy. After all, most people wouldn't be smiling that soft, pleased smile after watching someone eat a raw heart.

Maybe they could make it.

14

CALEB

Caleb had only vague memories of Jasper in the clearing. Jasper with glowing eyes and the cutest little horns, looking like the god Pan himself, bloody and . . . either glorious or just gory, it was hard to say, since he was delirious from blood loss.

He wasn't entirely sure it had happened, hadn't been a dream, but dreams weren't usually so painful.

The walk home was spotty, and he remembered falling against a few trees along the way, but somehow, he made it. They made it. Thank goodness the cabin door wasn't locked; he didn't think either of them could have managed a key in their state.

Jasper, despite being half dead, insisted that they clean up before curling up in bed together.

"To the bathroom," he rasped when Caleb headed for the bed. "We're both covered in blood. Don't want to get our nest all disgusting and bloody."

It was odd, a protest about blood coming from a man who had it smeared all over his face and body, but Caleb's only response had been an epic pouting session.

"Don't care," he mumbled.

Jasper tugged ineffectually on his arm. "You'll care when you wake up to your whole bed covered in blood and gore."

As much as Caleb didn't want to bother, that was true. Little flakes of dried blood would be impossible to get out of his huge blanket, and it didn't fit in the washing machine very well. He gave a deep sigh and let Jasper tug him along.

When they got into the bathroom, he planted himself on the edge of the tub and watched as Jasper searched through the cabinets, pulling out a fresh rag, a box of gauze strips, and a long Ace bandage Caleb hadn't even realized he had. Probably a holdover from the cabin's previous owner, since Caleb wasn't often in need of such things.

"Strip," Jasper ordered, as he himself started stripping out of his bloody clothes.

Caleb tried to do the same to himself, as hard as it was. His bloodless limbs didn't want to respond to simple commands, so it took him three tries to even lift his legs to slide the jeans over and off his feet.

Gently, so, so gently, Jasper wet the washrag and cleaned Caleb's chest, avoiding the worst of the claw marks the monster had left. It was nice. He put some kind of ointment on the gauze and wrapped the bandage around it all, and it hurt, but already had that annoying itchy sensation that meant it was healing.

Poppy would have been able to heal him—hell, if he were

more conscious, he could heal himself better—but she wouldn't have been so sweet or caring about it. This was more painful, but it was nicer.

It was Jasper.

He had to wring out the rag half a dozen times as he worked, first on Caleb, then on himself. Caleb wondered how much of the blood was his and how much the monster's.

Hard to complain though, since he was the one still alive. Maybe not standing, not yet, but he would get there.

He startled awake to Jasper touching his face. "We can go to bed now."

"Could've gone to bed hours ago," he mumbled petulantly.

Jasper reached down as though he would pull Caleb up, which would have been an impressive feat any day, and instead leaned forward, pressing his face into the crook of Caleb's neck and staying there.

He was falling asleep, too, Caleb realized, and forced himself awake enough to stand and guide Jasper toward the bed.

He glanced at Jasper's phone still sitting on the bedside table and a thought occurred to him. Poppy had been uselessly unavailable for days, but maybe—"We could call your siblings. Maybe they could help."

Jasper picked up the phone with trepidation on his face, picked a number, and dialed it. From the way he waited, then hung up, apparently there had been no answer. He bit his lip, stared at the phone screen for a moment, then shook his head and turned it off. After he set it back on the nightstand, though, he didn't move away, just kept looking at it.

"Didn't want to try anyone else?" Caleb asked.

Jasper jumped a little at the sound of his voice, then shook his head so vehemently he almost tipped over. Caleb barely caught him, and even Jasper's tiny weight made him tip as well. Fortunately, they were right next to the bed, so with a little effort, he made sure they landed there.

"You sure?" he asked, though the answer didn't seem to matter nearly as much as spooning up against Jasper's back, trying to warm his freezing extremities. The pressure against his aching chest wasn't his favorite thing, but now that he was safe and the bleeding had stopped, his healing was accelerating. He just needed a very good night's sleep, and half the food in his refrigerator, and he'd be okay.

Jasper snuggled his face into the pillow, and his back against Caleb. "Declan might have, but the rest . . . their kind of help isn't . . . no. They wouldn't help."

Caleb thought maybe he heard a silent "you" attached to the end of that statement, but he understood. Sometimes even when it was well intentioned, family wasn't that helpful. His and Poppy's fae mother would kill Jasper to help Caleb and not feel the least bit bad about it. Fortunately for the two of them, their human father had taught them a little better.

Caleb didn't know anything about Jasper's family life. For all he knew, the reputation demons had was correct for everyone except Jasper. Maybe they would come and insist Jasper eat Caleb. That didn't seem like an ideal end to what had already been a difficult day.

He didn't try to press for answers. They should be fine. Caleb just needed time and food, and Jasper had gotten what he needed to heal, right?

He roused enough to look down at the younger man, already mostly asleep, blond lashes fanned across too-pale, hollow cheeks.

Jasper didn't look a lot better. He had managed to get to Caleb, somehow, and to get back, but it wouldn't have helped him, trekking through the forest practically carrying his giant useless ass.

Still, there was a little more color in his cheeks than there had been. And if he was an incubus, what he really needed was for Caleb to get better and give him a proper meal.

Caleb settled down and smiled into the back of Jasper's neck. He couldn't lie to himself, he was kind of looking forward to that. Jasper had been so sweet, so perfect the first time. It could only get better as he got healthier. Right?

15

JASPER

Jasper woke to the sound of crunching. After they'd cleaned up the night before, he hadn't bothered putting clothes back on. He liked Caleb's soft T-shirts, how they were so long they hung halfway down his thighs and how they smelled like him, but it was too much effort to pull open another drawer. Seven hells, it was only Caleb's maneuvering that'd let them fall into bed instead of sprawled out on the floor.

If they'd fallen, Jasper didn't know that he would have gotten up again.

Scowling, he rolled over and looked up to see Caleb standing there, a bag of baby carrots in his hand. He popped another into his mouth and chewed.

"Carrot?" He stuck the bag out.

Jasper frowned. "No, thanks."

Caleb gave it a little jiggle, and his cocked brow was cute

enough that Jasper relented, reaching in to grab just one. He ate it.

"I got you a water." Caleb nodded at the glass on the side table.

"Thanks?" It wasn't that surprising that Caleb was trying to take care of him, but he said it like a glass of water were both obvious and meaningful on its own. "How are you feeling?"

With a scowl, Caleb rubbed his palm over his bandaged chest. "Itchy," he admitted.

Jasper smiled. Itchy meant healing. If he could gripe about that, he was going to be fine.

Considering that they'd spent the last night in bed, Caleb recovering from a bear attack, the big guy seemed in a weirdly good mood. He finished off the bag of carrots, balled it up, and dropped it on the night table.

For a second, Jasper watched him. He hadn't bothered with pants, and . . . well, who could blame him for staring? Caleb was perfect. He was soft where Jasper wanted to grab onto him, and heavy and muscled in a way that made Jasper think he could move mountains. He had the kind of body Jasper wanted pressing down on top of him. And he was so fucking hungry.

When he met Caleb's eyes again, only after dragging his gaze up Caleb's furry stomach and chest, Caleb smirked. "Anything on the menu you'd like to order?"

Jasper's breath caught as Caleb's hand slid down to palm his own cock, stroking it to hardness. His mouth watered, and he keened and reached for Caleb. He dragged his hand up the back of Caleb's thigh and pulled.

"If you're not up to it—" Caleb's smile faltered for a second.

Jasper ran his tongue over his lips and looked up at him. "You said you know what I am?"

"Yeah."

"Then you know I'm up for it." Jasper's voice had turned into a low rasp. His fingers clenched on Caleb's ass, and his big bear man let him pull him in as he shifted to the edge of the bed.

He brushed his wet lips over Caleb's cock head. The man's breath punched out of him, and Jasper smiled before sliding down on his cock, pushing until the thick, blunt head hit the back of his throat. He groaned, and under his grip, Caleb flexed his hips.

When he pulled back, he circled his tongue, teasing his slit with the tip. Jasper chased taste of him, tracing the ridges of muscle and vein like he could take Caleb apart with only his mouth to win his sweet prize.

Still exhausted and holding himself at a strange angle on his propped elbow, it was a relief when Caleb's fingers twined in his golden hair.

Jasper dropped his head to the mattress and let Caleb take over, his cock rounding his cheek. He looked up to see Caleb's face had flushed, his pupils blown wide in his intense eyes. Minutely, he nodded, and Caleb held him down with a fist in his hair and the weight of his palm's heel as he fucked Jasper's mouth.

"Fuck, baby," Caleb hissed. "So good. So fucking good."

Short, quick thrusts had Jasper's skin blazing with heat. His throat convulsed, swallowing around Caleb's thick cock. It *was* so good. Salty and bitter and perfect, but better still was the undercurrent of thrumming pleasure he felt from Caleb. It built, first a thread wrapped Jasper's around heart, then a fist. It squeezed, Jasper's heart lurched, and he pulled back with a gasp.

Caleb let him go at once. His ruddy, swollen lips parted on heavy breaths. Jasper whined as his heart pulsed. Fuck, he hadn't realized how weak he'd been.

"I need you," he rasped before Caleb could ask if he was okay. He was so, so okay. "Now. Please."

Caleb's broad hands curled around his ribs, pulling him closer. Then he was gripping Jasper's hips. His fingers dug in to keep Jasper from straining down, chasing exquisite friction against Caleb's skin. Like he was nothing, Caleb flipped him over with his legs bent and pressed against the mattress at the edge of the bed.

Utterly exposed with his ass arched upward, Jasper whimpered. He twisted his fingers in the sheets and curled his toes as Caleb slicked his fingers. He pushed one in with no warning, and Jasper whined, working back on his hand.

"There," Jasper panted when Caleb curled his finger. "There, oh god."

Caleb made quick work of prepping him, scissoring his fingers open until Jasper was trembling at the feel of cool air on his entrance. He needed the thick, hot steel heat of Caleb's cock.

"Please, Caleb, I—"

With a soft hiss, Caleb quieted him. His rough hands spread Jasper wide, then the blunt head of his cock pressed in.

"Oh fuck," Jasper whimpered as Caleb filled him in one slow, relentless thrust.

His hands slid up Jasper's back, pressing him down into the bed and holding him prone. When his fingers curled around Jasper's shoulders, he pulled out and thrust back in. Hard.

Jasper cried out, flinging one hand back to squeeze Caleb into him. "S—so deep," he stammered. "So perfect. Caleb—"

"I've got you," Caleb swore, his thumbs brushing the back of Jasper's strained neck.

The force of his thrusts unlodged one of Jasper's legs. His toes touched the floor, and he arched up to meet Caleb's pounding hips. The sounds that came out of him were unholy, but he couldn't think of a single damn thing except Caleb fucking him so good and the tingling swell of Caleb's pleasure.

It felt amazing, to know how much Caleb wanted this. Overwhelming.

One of Caleb's hands slipped under his chest and pulled him back. His shoulders hit Caleb's chest, and the man grunted. His callused fingers pressed flat against Jasper's collarbone. With one hand, he held Jasper there and rocked into him, their bodies flush.

With the other, he reached down. All he did was curl his fingers around Jasper's aching cock, and when he thrust, he rocked Jasper forward into that grip and the delicious drag of his rough skin, soon coated in Jasper's precome.

When Caleb came, the force of it hit Jasper like a tidal wave. His teeth dug into Jasper's neck again, and fuck if that wasn't the hottest thing Jasper'd ever felt, like Caleb was claiming him.

Crying Caleb's name, he spilled against the side of the bed in thick, hot streams as Caleb pumped inside him.

The thread of Caleb's arousal was still there, wrapped around his heart, now a steady stream. Trembling in Caleb's arms, too weak and overwhelmed to hold himself up on his own legs, he drank and drank as Caleb's body gave him so much.

In the end, Caleb had to pick him up and settle him back on the bed. Jasper whined as Caleb slid out of him, but a moment later, Caleb collapsed on the bed against his side.

Laying on one arm, he reached out and ran a hand down Jasper's chest. "How do you feel?"

Jasper couldn't help smiling. Even the worry in Caleb's eyes wasn't enough to keep him from grinning like a mad man.

"So *full*, Caleb," he whispered.

He took a deep breath and leaned in to brush his lips across Caleb's. His mouth was still cool from the carrots, and sweet. With a gentle, persistent push, he turned Caleb onto his back and crawled on top of him. As he let his hands explore Caleb's arms and shoulders, his tongue mapped Caleb's mouth. Straddling his waist, Jasper rocked lazily.

Caleb broke the kiss with a soft laugh. "You might have to let me rest a second."

Jasper leaned up so he could look down at Caleb's handsome face. Biting his lip, he shook his head.

"As long as you can get it up, we can go all day. And I'm patient, Caleb. I'll get you there." He gripped Caleb's hands. "Then, I'm gonna drain you dry."

A moan fell from Caleb's lips, and Jasper didn't think he minded the sound of that so much.

16

CALEB

Caleb had lost track of how many times they'd fucked. Jasper hadn't been kidding; as long as Caleb had the strength to keep going, Jasper could get him up. Hell, he imagined that Jasper could get him up even if he didn't, but fortunately, his little incubus was one of the good guys.

The result had been a dozen or more meals, since he was feeding both himself and Jasper, who took from him. As long as his stomach didn't explode, it was an excellent answer to everyone's problems.

Heck, it wasn't like Caleb minded eating a little more than usual. It helped a lot that the sex was better than any he'd had before. He'd just never thought the phrase "feeding him my cock" would be quite so on the nose.

"You can stop if you want, you know," Jasper told him with a chuckle as he poured macaroni and cheese into a bowl.

Caleb grinned back at him, then turned to the sink and rinsed out the pan before setting it in the dishwasher. "You kidding? How often does a guy get an excuse to eat ten thousand calories in a day?"

Jasper's chuckle turned into a full-blown laugh. He turned to dig through the fridge, pulling out a fresh bag of carrot sticks and holding them out. "At least have something vaguely healthy along with your bowl of heart disease."

He grabbed a handful of them and added them to a plate of crackers he'd been munching on while cooking, then shoved one into his mouth, crunching down. "Are you sure you don't need anything?"

Jasper blushed and shook his head. He'd put his hair up to keep it out of the way for the most spectacular blowjob Caleb had ever gotten, but since their last round, drifting locks of light blond had come free and brushed his cheeks. Caleb didn't hesitate to brush one behind his ear just to feel the warmth of that flushed cheek.

"I, um, don't really need to eat anything," Jasper admitted.

"So I bought you all those cookies and didn't get to eat any, for no reason?" He stuck out his lip in a parody of a pout. "At least leave me one next time?"

Jasper's smile went soft, and he nodded. His words belied the softness though. "One it is."

He squealed in delight when Caleb jumped up from his seat at the counter and chased him over to the bed, tickling his ribs until he threw up his hands in supplication. "Fine, fine, you win!"

Caleb pulled back and looked at him, waiting.

"You can have two." He laughed maniacally when Caleb reached in to tickle him some more.

"I'll give you two cookies, you little monster."

By the time he got back to his macaroni, he needed to put it in the microwave to reheat it. Microwaved macaroni wasn't his favorite thing, but it didn't matter so much when Jasper sat on his lap while he ate it.

It probably made Caleb weak or soft, that his favorite position of the day was their last. Precisely the way they'd been sleeping for the whole week, they lay on their sides, Jasper in front of him, ass pressed into Caleb's groin.

Just, this time, Caleb was lazily fucking him as they did so.

He thought Jasper was half asleep, so he slowed his strokes. He didn't really need to get off again. It had been more than half a dozen times when he lost count, and he was only still going for Jasper's sake.

Just as he stopped altogether, Jasper made a weak noise of protest. "M'not asleep."

"You sure?" he asked.

Jasper gave a huge yawn, but nodded anyway and mumbled, "More."

So he lay there, one arm wrapped around Jasper's slender chest, sliding into him over and over, murmuring softly in his ear. "Do you have any idea how beautiful you are like this? How perfect?"

That earned him a sleepy smile, and Jasper turned his head to look at him. "Me? Dunno how you can say that when you're all . . . you-y."

"Me-y?"

With some difficulty, Jasper got his arm out from under himself and twisted it around to cup Caleb's cheek, then card softly through his beard. "You-y," he affirmed. "In the manner of being you, or something like that."

Caleb slid the arm he had wrapped around Jasper's chest up to caress his cheek and turn it that extra inch toward him, and pushed their lips together.

"Not sure how I made it through before I had you here to define these things for me."

Jasper slitted one eye open, unimpressed. "Easy. You just didn't know what things meant then."

On that, they could entirely agree.

"Maybe not." Caleb leaned in to capture his lips again. "Probably not."

"Definitely not. You know that one, right?"

"There's another one you taught me," Caleb told him, keeping his tone light and playful.

Jasper opened the other eye, expression dubious, but willing to listen. "What's that?"

Caleb slid deep inside him, pressing one last kiss to his lips as he came. After the wildness of the whole day, it wasn't an electric thing, but a soft one, just like the kiss. He closed his eyes and pressed their cheeks together, whispering, "I love you."

Jasper's breath caught for a moment, then he let out a broken whimper, tightening his grip on Caleb and whispering, "I love you too."

JASPER

Caleb loved him.

Caleb *loved* him.

And Jasper loved him back.

It'd been easy to say, as Caleb held him and fed him gently. By that point, Jasper was sated. He just liked being close to Caleb. And shit, he'd almost died. A little life-affirming sex was fair game, right?

As soon as Jasper was up to it, though, they'd spent an entire day in bed. It was just one day, but Jasper was perfectly content to let Caleb eat every single thing in the fridge and get right back to it.

And it'd been perfect. Not just the sex, but Caleb tickling his sides, smiling at him, being so happy.

But then he thought about the people Malcolm brought home, and how glassy-eyed they'd get after a day or so in his company. And the thralls Elrith kept around to suit his fancy.

And how it was practically impossible for anyone to break out of an incubus's hold.

So, yeah, Jasper loved Caleb. He loved him too much to hurt him like that, and he'd proven it was in his nature to be selfish with him. After all Caleb had done for him, Jasper could always take more.

"Hey." Jasper shifted under the blankets on the couch and nudged Caleb's thigh with his foot. Caleb was eating a bowl of cereal. He'd already gone through all the eggs in the house, most of the lunch meat and cheese and grapes and a truly startling number of carrot sticks.

They were sitting on the couch, watching *The Princess Bride*. And like every other damn thing with Caleb, it was achingly wonderful.

"Yeah?" When Caleb looked at him, his hazel eyes were soft. He was a little gruff sometimes, sure, but he was pretty good with his words too. And still, his eyes were what convinced Jasper that Caleb meant it when he said he loved him.

How long would it be before Caleb didn't have a choice? He'd look at Jasper, just as glassy eyed and empty as the rest, while Jasper used him. Over and over, because that was what he was— a demon who used people.

"I want some Oreos," Jasper said, nibbling his bottom lip.

"Oh, baby wants some cookies?" Caleb teased. He set his bowl aside and leaned over Jasper's legs to squeeze his sides. "I don't know where they go."

Jasper grinned. "They're what makes me so damn sweet."

"Ah." Caleb leaned in then, like he just had to see for himself.

His lips were a soft press against Jasper's. When he opened, Caleb's tongue swept into his mouth, and Jasper sighed. "Yeah. Pretty damn sweet."

With a light shove, Jasper cocked a brow at him. "And your fridge is practically empty."

"Mmkay," Caleb shrugged. "I'll go later."

Right then, it seemed he couldn't be bothered. He sank forward, dropping his head on Jasper's chest and turning to watch the TV. He stayed there, not pushing down hard, but a warm, firm weight on top of him. And for once, all they did was watch the movie.

There Westley was, right on the screen, promising Buttercup anything. "As you wish," he said, not because her magic or her nature demanded he bend to please her, but because he wanted to. He loved her. Simple and human.

As Jasper combed his fingers through Caleb's thick hair, holding him through witches who weren't witches but wives, and adventures and revenge, he wished more than anything that he were simple and human too.

LATER, after Caleb got dressed to go to the store, Jasper had a moment's panic. He didn't have much to take with him. He'd put his clothes back on—his jeans stained with blood, but clean from going through the wash again. His keys were by his phone on the nightstand, his car useless and forgotten in the woods. When he left, there'd be nothing left of him here but some rumpled sheets, and Caleb would have those clean soon enough.

But he couldn't stay—Caleb was too good for Jasper to turn him into a snack, hollow him out, drain him dry.

And as much as Jasper didn't want to hurt him, his instincts demanded it. He hadn't *wanted* to get out of bed the day before. He'd been all too happy to watch Caleb eat and eat and eat so he could take what he wanted.

It wasn't right, and Caleb deserved better.

But he couldn't just *leave*. On the table sat Caleb's note from when he'd gone after the monster. Jasper swallowed, blinking a little too fast, when he read it again.

Love, Caleb.

Fuck.

He flipped it over and scrawled a quick note on the back.

I really do love you. Enjoy the Oreos for me.
   Jasper

It wasn't enough—wasn't enough by such a wide margin that Jasper felt sick. But now that he was better, he couldn't have this. It sucked, that surviving meant he didn't deserve the only thing that'd gotten him through it. But incubi didn't settle down. They couldn't have just one person, not forever, not without—

He couldn't think about it. Caleb would be better off without him. He grabbed his keys, shoved them in his jeans, and set out for the hike back to his car.

18

CALEB

It was the strangest sensation; Caleb didn't think he'd felt it in years. Maybe not ever.

He was whistling.

He had a spring in his step, and despite the fact that the weather was all wrong, it suddenly felt like spring. Sure, there was still snow here and there, and the ground was more wet and muddy than lush and green, but the snow was melting and the birds were singing, and by the gods, Caleb was in love.

He pulled two bags out of the back of his car, making sure one of them held the Oreos, and headed for the front door.

Jasper wasn't in the main room of the cabin, though.

The bathroom door was open.

The loft window that led out onto the roof was closed.

Jasper's clothes were gone. Not the shirts of Caleb's he'd been wearing most of the week, but his own stylish jeans and brand new hiking boots, and . . .

It took half an hour for him to find the note.

THERE WAS a cliff half a mile from the cabin, overlooking a beautiful vista of pine trees and a distant snow-capped mountain. It was maybe fifty yards from top to bottom. Plenty far enough to kill a man if he fell off it.

Caleb sat on the edge, looking down.

He tore open the second package of cookies and tossed the first one over the edge.

"Enjoy the Oreos," he muttered to himself, pulling another from the tray and throwing it as hard as he could. "I don't even like Oreos."

Far below him, a bird hopped out of the trees and circled the fallen cookie. It started to break pieces off in its beak, and Caleb spared a thought to whether chocolate was bad for forest creatures.

None of them would get that much of it—they'd be fine.

He threw another one.

"I."

"Hate."

"Cookies."

"Oh, then can I have them?" Poppy's bright voice came from behind him.

He whipped around so fast that he didn't even think about it before loosing a cookie in her direction.

She, of course, caught it. "Thanks!"

"Really? *Really?*"

With her most innocent expression, all wide eyes and smooth brow, she watched him and waited, peeling her damned cookie apart and licking the greasy white filling.

"You just happened to be missing for a week, and you show back up the second everything's"—he looked away from her, ripping another cookie out of the bag and throwing it—"everything's over."

"Oh my gods, Cay, seriously? 'Everything's over'? Tell me this scene is for melodramatic for effect." Seeming not the least bit bothered, she sauntered over and planted herself next to him, taking the next cookie before he could toss it. "You're being ridiculous."

"How would you possibly know what I'm *being?*" He turned to her, glaring, and dumped the rest of the cookies in the bag over the edge all at once.

She frowned as she watched them fall, and looked back up at him, brows knit together. "That was just unnecessary. Pastry-cide?"

"Oreos are not pastries."

"You should save the rest of those. You really should." When he moved to grab the next package out of the bag, she threw up a hand in front of him. "Give the kid a break, little brother. He's the son of a giant fucking douchebag who goes through humans the way some people go through underwear."

That did give Caleb a moment's pause. Jasper had said something about it. That his family wouldn't help if called.

"His sister Sasha is a good egg, too, but she needs more help than him." Poppy gave a dreamy smile, and the kind of help she wanted to give Sasha was readily apparent. "Really, though. Give him a break. I mean, he *loves you*, doesn't he?"

Caleb glared at his sister. "Did you know every single thing that happened this week? I could have died, you know."

She waved him away dismissively. "You can handle one dark forest spirit." Hopping up, she leaned over and kissed him on top of the head. "You needed to defeat the big bad bear who had lost touch with his humanity. And now you can go forth into a bright future of sexing up your adorable little twinkubus."

He stared at her, openmouthed, as she darted around him and grabbed the next bag of cookies. "Do you even hear yourself?"

"I do. I mean, there's a reason I'm the social one. I say sensible things that people should hear. I don't just growl and waste cookies." She ruffled his hair. "I texted you his address. He won't be hard to find."

She left him alone with two remaining bags of cookies and his thoughts.

If Jasper really loved him, like he'd said, why had he run off? He had to know that he didn't have to do what his father did. If one had to follow in their parents' footsteps, Caleb and Poppy would have been wandering the countryside, kidnapping humans to use as slaves.

So Jasper had to know.

Didn't he?

19

JASPER

"You look better," Sasha said, perching on the edge of Jasper's bed. She reached over and shoved his hip when he didn't move.

All Jasper could do was grunt and shrug. He was better. Physically, he was fine for the first time in months. If he didn't get out of bed, that might change. But who cared? He'd had his perfect moment—more than any demon ever deserved.

"You said you met someone?" Sasha hedged at his lack of response. That vague allusion alone had Jasper's memory flooding with Caleb's smile and the weight of his arm, always ready to loop around his waist and pull him close. With a shaking inhale, he braced against the shattering of his heart.

He dragged his gaze up to meet Sasha's. She was smiling hopefully down at him, her long brown fingers sweeping his hair back from his temple.

His breath hitched. "Yeah."

"You gonna tell me about him?"

What was there to tell? Caleb was tall and strong and handsome and kind. He'd picked Jasper up off the ground and nursed him back to health. Even when he hadn't felt the demon's tug, he'd kissed Jasper sweetly, and when he was recovering from his fight, he'd still held Jasper against his chest while they slept.

He was so good—everything Jasper'd ever wanted—and Jasper would only ever hurt him. Take from him and give nothing back.

"Oh, hun," she whispered as his lips started to tremble. Those two syllables were too much. He turned his face into his pillow and let it soak up his tears.

He'd been home for a day, and he hadn't gotten out of bed. He could've. This wasn't the exhaustion of starving; it was worse—he was heartbroken.

For a long time, she just combed her fingers through his hair. When she finally broke the silence, she asked, "Was he at least tall?"

Jasper didn't know why, but a hoarse laugh escaped him and he lifted his head again. "Big as a bear."

Sasha chuckled and wiped tears off his cheek. "Least we know you haven't compromised your standards. So . . . what happened? We both know he didn't turn you away."

Right. Because people didn't do that to incubi. They couldn't. Maybe Caleb thought he loved him now, but what if one day, that changed? Caleb would want him to go, want his freedom from his leeching demon boyfriend, and he wouldn't be able to say it. Hell, maybe he wouldn't even be able to place what made him so unhappy.

Jasper rolled onto his side and shrugged his top shoulder. "I just didn't want to hurt him," he whispered.

Pursing her lips, Sasha scowled. "Sweetie," she said after a moment, weighing her words carefully, "that's not you."

He didn't miss a beat. "It's all of us."

It wasn't the easiest thing in the world, to hate what he was—worse that he couldn't share why. When he'd accidentally seduced his straight best friend, it was just what incubi did. Try explaining to Malcolm that just because he could have someone didn't make it okay.

Lying in bed crying was definitely not conducive to weighing the ethics of various demonic activity. "How's Declan?"

The weight of her concern shifted off him, and he could breathe again. "What do you mean?"

"I . . . tried calling him while I was away. He didn't pick up." That wasn't like Declan at all, really. He was reliable as anyone, almost always at home alone, only had company when he paid for it. In fact, the only reason he still lived in the same building as them was to keep an eye out for them. He'd stayed to "offer an alternative to Elrith's bullshit." Declan thought being the youngest of Elrith's spawn also made them the most vulnerable —a position that regularly boiled Malcolm's temper.

Sasha only shrugged. "I didn't really notice when he left, you know? I was kind of worried about you." Guiltily, she grimaced. "But I'm sure he's just out doing his ocean thing! He'll be back."

Jasper chewed his lip. "Fair enough."

Sometimes, Declan had to go out and see the sea. Jasper didn't get it, but if his time in Poisonwood had taught him anything, it was that there were better places to live than Lyric.

Malcolm knocked on the door, and Jasper started. Before either of them answered, he stuck his head in. "Dad knows you're home. He's coming over."

Jasper flinched. Elrith would want an explanation—where he'd gone, why he hadn't dropped everything and come to dinner when he called. Elrith might have only called them together to announce his purchase of a new pair of merino wool socks, but if he'd put the effort into summoning them, he expected appeasement. This wasn't a friendly visit; it was an inspection.

Sasha had to nudge him out of bed anyway. He didn't *think* his father would rip his heart out of his chest and eat it in front of them if he continued to laze around, but what the hell did he know, really? No reason to test America's richest demon dad.

He got dressed—not in the jeans he'd been wearing for the better part of a week. Those were in his laundry hamper, shoved deep down so he could try and forget the electric scrape of Caleb's hands as he peeled them off him. Instead, he pulled out slacks, a button up, nice shoes. His Sunday best, if he were allowed on hallowed ground. When he looked in the mirror, he looked like a slight, golden Malcolm.

Brilliant.

While they waited for Elrith, he, Sasha, and Malcolm perched uneasily in the living room. At a sharp, precise knock on the door, Malcolm was the first to dart out of his seat, but they all stood.

"I've got it," Malcolm muttered. The only time Jasper ever heard him sound unsure was when confronted by their father's impatience.

There was always pressure to keep the apartment clean, springing from the fact that Elrith did, in fact, pay for the place and could show up any time.

"Malcolm," Elrith snapped before stepping past him. Jasper fought the urge to fidget with his clothes. After a week in Caleb's cozy shirts and sweatpants, a button-up and a belt were practically torture devices.

Elrith looked around at their apartment first, like he might find a speck of dust to gripe about before he moved onto all his other disappointments. But no dust bunny was half as grating to him as Jasper was.

"So you're back," Elrith drawled as his startlingly bright gaze locked on him. Jasper had his mother's eyes, more gray than blue and common and, well, he liked to think they were nicer in that they weren't so goddamn creepy.

Awkwardly, Jasper's lips twitched into an uncomfortable smile.

Elrith looked like Jasper, but taller and broader—a fact that struck him hard as his father stepped close enough to intimidate. He smelled like expensive cologne, and his thick blond hair was styled so it swept back from his face to expose a hard, classic jawline.

Malcolm had Elrith's eyes, his shape, and his sneer, but Jasper liked to think he was jealous of the gold hair—he should be. Even inside, it had a striking sheen.

"So I'm back." Jasper's shoulders jerked up. He wasn't quite bold enough to be outright rebellious. Never had been.

Unimpressed, Elrith grabbed his chin and turned it up. "Well," he said after a moment's inspection, "at least you're eating again."

Jasper's stomach rolled as Elrith dropped his hand.

"And on that happy note," Elrith continued. "I thought we might have a family dinner night."

"Brilliant idea, Father," Malcolm gushed. "It's been too long since we've had a proper hunt."

Elrith watched for Jasper's flinch, and he wasn't disappointed. A slow smirk unbalanced his lips.

"Oh, I can't," Jasper blurted. He could—he always could—but . . . no. Never again. Especially not with the aching stretch of Caleb's cock inside him so close to his thoughts. "I'm full. Honestly, so full. You couldn't *imagine* how full."

Sasha's mouth fell open, and even then, she was grinning to hear him say it. She squeezed Jasper's forearm.

"That's right. Jasper's been feasting on bear for a week. But I'll go out with you," she offered sweetly, rocking onto the balls of her feet.

Elrith scowled, and Malcolm looked equally unimpressed, but Sasha linked her arms with theirs. When Malcolm mentioned a new club opening, they left without him. Though not before Elrith made a foreboding comment about "next time."

Jasper tried not to sigh at the overblown menace in the

words. Everything about his father was exhausting, and he just wanted another nap.

20

CALEB

The address was in his phone, and thank goodness for that. Caleb never would have found the high-rise apartment on his own. Bears weren't exactly trackers, and his sense of smell wasn't up to the task.

He wanted to think he could find Jasper anywhere, but it obviously wasn't true.

He wasn't even sure he knew Jasper like he'd thought.

What if it had all been a ruse?

He glanced down at the bag of godsdamned Oreos in his hands, and almost dropped them into the nearest trash can. Instead, he steeled his spine, drew himself to his full height, and marched up to the elevator.

"Floor?" asked the snooty attendant. He was looking Caleb over and had clearly already found him wanting.

Caleb met his eyes, staring hard, and gave him the floor number.

The man looked like he wanted to protest, but apparently the scary guy in front of him trumped the scary rich guy who might eat his soul.

Did incubi eat souls? Caleb's knowledge of them was lacking, and frankly, if Jasper didn't want him, he had no interest in learning any more. He had no need of an incubus in a general way. Sex with Jasper had been incredible, but that had been because it was Jasper, not because of some demonic sex powers.

The elevator stopped and the man looked at him, waiting, smirking, like maybe Caleb would have changed his mind. Caleb blinked, shook himself out of his reverie, and stepped off the elevator, giving the man his back and no attention.

The hallway was fancier than anything in Caleb's cabin. There was a table in marbled wood, with an enormous display of fresh flowers in garish red and black. Caleb couldn't think of anything that suited Jasper less, but he reminded himself that maybe he didn't know Jasper at all.

Maybe Jasper belonged in this place more than he belonged in the cabin.

He knocked on the door and waited, head down, staring at the cookies. He shouldn't have brought them. It was silly.

Gods, he hated Oreos so much.

The door opened on Jasper saying, "Don't tell me you forgot your keys." When he saw Caleb, he froze. "You—"

Caleb took him in, in his fancy clothes, hair straight and neat, wearing leather loafers instead of his ridiculous hiking boots. "You—" Caleb's voice came out raspy and strained, so he cleared his throat and tried again. "You asked me to bring you these."

Jasper's gaze fell to the cookies and stayed there for a long moment. He bit his lip, and Caleb wanted nothing more than to lean in and kiss him breathless. He didn't like the fancy clothes; they weren't *his* Jasper, but they did look beautiful on him.

Anything would look perfect on Jasper. Almost as perfect as nothing at all.

"This is so ridiculous. Who carries a wallet in this day and age?" an affected, nasally voice huffed from Caleb's right, and he looked over to see a dark-haired man flouncing down the hall. He marched right up to Caleb and only then seemed to notice his existence. "Move, creature," he ordered.

Caleb simply stood there and stared at him until he got huffy and shoved past.

"Honestly, Jasper," the man called over his shoulder. "Grow some balls and just tell him you're not interested in whatever it is he's selling. It's probably a scam anyway."

Jasper winced, and his reaction to the idea of summoning his family made a lot more sense. Caleb thought Poppy was hard to explain to people, but at least most of the time Poppy wasn't intentionally an ass.

Except when she was leaving him to handle the Poisonwood monster on his own.

"I—I can't really—" Jasper muttered, without looking up to meet Caleb's eye. "I'm sorry. But I'm not—you're not—"

"Oh for fuck's sake, Jasper," the man said, marching back into the room as he stuffed a wallet into his pocket. He stopped and looked down, then huffed again and rolled his eyes. "Honestly, this completely ruins the line of my trousers."

"It's a wallet," Jasper muttered. "If you're going clubbing, you should probably have money."

The man waved him off. "As though I ever have to pay for anything. Father insisted, though." He looked back over at Caleb, giving him the slimiest once over he'd ever been subjected to in his life. He wanted to take two showers after that. Then the man got a nasty smile on his face and turned to Jasper. "Oh, Jas."

"Malcolm—" Jasper started, but the man cut him off.

"When Sasha said you spent the week fucking a bear, I was worried she'd meant the actual woodland creature."

Caleb's stomach dropped, his blood going cold. Jasper had told these people about him? He'd told this man?

The man looked over at him again, and somehow, the gaze grew even more disturbing. It was almost like a physical thing, oily and heavy and intrusive. When he was finished, he turned up his nose. "Honestly, Jasper, you'd have been better off with the animal. At least it wouldn't smell like that."

He took the bag of cookies from Caleb's hands and tossed them into a trash can near the door, then closed it in Caleb's face.

There were raised voices behind the door, but it didn't matter anymore. Jasper had told everyone about him.

He'd spent the week having sex with a bear.

That was all he was to Jasper, then. A week of sex.

He turned and headed for the elevator, but thought better of it and took the stairs. He didn't need to face the snooty elevator attendant on the way down too.

Fucking Oreos.

21

JASPER

When Jasper had wrenched the door open again, Caleb was gone. Of course he was. Confronted with the knowledge of what Jasper really was, how could he do anything but leave?

Malcolm left too, and good fucking riddance. It meant Jasper was alone to fall apart.

He fished the Oreos out of the trash and sat down on the fine leather sofa—treated leather, of course, because you could just wipe it off. He grimaced. But that wasn't the point. With shaky hands, he opened the pack of Oreos.

He'd never bothered counting them before. There'd always been the prospect of more, but there wouldn't be more from Caleb.

Thirty-nine. And now that the pack was open, he'd be lucky if the cookies stayed fresh for more than a week or so. Still, he could stand a couple stale cookies.

He'd eat three a day. One for breakfast, one for lunch, and one for dinner. Make them last.

He picked out his first one, twisted the cookies apart, and ate top and bottom separately, just to spread it out.

JASPER HAD GOTTEN halfway through his pack of Oreos when he started to get hungry again. The real kind of hungry.

He wasn't sure he would've cared, except Caleb had tried so hard to make him well. He'd killed an enormous monster and fought for him, and Jasper couldn't just throw that effort away.

He dragged his ass back to Silverstone's Emporium, trusting that Sasha hadn't read Poppy wrong and the whole thing with the flowers had been a big misunderstanding. Leaving the apartment meant showering and making himself presentable for the first time in days. It was exhausting.

The bell above the door jingled when he entered, and Poppy Silverstone came out of the back. She stood there, staring, and Jasper's feet glued to the spot as she started to glare.

"Ah, you." She pursed her lips and crossed her arms. "Sorry, but I'm done with your whole"—she waved her hand down his body—"sad, suffering, twinkubus bullshit. We're closed."

Jasper blinked. "I'm—I'm sorry?"

He expected the world to be disgusted with him, but he didn't hear it out loud often. And she'd been so ready to help the last time he'd been there, even if her advice was unhelpful. Jasper was completely willing to accept that he'd eaten the wrong flower, done something the wrong way, somehow made the whole poison fiasco entirely his fault.

Of course, maybe she'd hated him from the start—had wanted him poisoned—and Sasha had been wrong the whole time. Hell, plenty of people had valid reasons for hating incubi.

"Listen, if I've—if I've done something to offend you, I'm really sorry, Ms. Silverstone." He shoved his hands in his pockets and shrank into his rounded shoulders.

That only made her madder. Hands braced on the counter, she leaned toward him like those few inches would be enough that her glare would catch him on fire.

"You're sorry? I sent you out into the woods, gave you a shot at *everything*, and here you are back again for—what? Baby incubus is hungee?" For the last, she used a cold, high, mocking voice.

He had no idea what he'd done, but he shrank further under her anger. "I'm sorry. The flowers didn't work. They, uh, they made me sick and—"

"Yeah, and you'd have been *fine* if you hadn't shoved half a dozen in your mouth. They just suppress your, you know, pheromones or whatever. Doesn't feel *great*. Might make you sick. But if you'd just eaten one, it'd have worn off in a day."

Okay, so maybe she hadn't been trying to kill him.

"I'm sorry," he blurted again. "Just, one day wasn't going to fix—"

"It wasn't about one day!"

Was she mad because he'd messed up? He hadn't hurt anyone but himself. Well, himself and—

"Caleb tried with you," she hissed. "He really tried. And do you have any idea how hard that is for him? How rare? And he didn't do it because of your demonic whatever, or your stupid pretty face—he did it because he's good. And he's fucking lonely. And I am the idiot who thought you were different because you're *sad*." Her face had turned a scary, pale white, her eyes flashing like she could open a hole in the fabric of the universe and chuck him through. "Well, now he's sad. And you, Jasper Jones—you can go and fuck yourself."

Jasper stood there, gaping at her. Her glare didn't let up, but he didn't know what to say. "I'm so sorry," he whispered, again, like that meant anything to anyone.

He rushed out of the shop, got in his car, and sped home. By the time he got into the flat, he was shaking.

For a long time, he sat there with his hands curled around the steering wheel. He didn't know why Poppy Silverstone cared about Caleb, but it didn't matter. She was right. He definitely didn't deserve her help.

There were too many people on the sidewalk. Slowly, Jasper's hunger came back—a thrumming ache he wanted nothing to do with. He forced himself back into their building, up the elevator, to their apartment.

"Fucking hell, are you starving yourself again?" Malcolm asked from the couch, his feet kicked up on the coffee table, when Jasper let himself in.

Jasper didn't have words. He rushed to his room and threw himself on the bed.

A minute later, or maybe an hour, there was a soft knock on

the door. He grunted. He didn't want company, even Sasha's, but she slipped inside anyway.

"Hey," she whispered. The bed sank with her weight, and she touched his shoulder. "Tell me what's going on?"

"I fucked everything up," he mumbled into his pillow.

"Okay, couldn't hear that. You're gonna have to—"

He lifted his head. "I fucked everything up."

That, the whole world deserved to hear.

"That's hard to believe. You're a little too sweet to go fucking up *everything*, Jas. What happened?"

Before he knew what he was doing, because she was his sister, he was spouting out the whole story—the flowers, how Caleb had picked him up and nursed him back to health, how hard he'd fought, how kind he'd been, and how Jasper had left him anyway.

"I don't know how we—how we can *be* with someone, Sasha. I don't want to hurt him. I don't want him to go all glassy eyed and empty. I love him the way he is now. I just—"

She grabbed his shoulder and pushed him back, so he had to look at her. "You listen to me, Jasper, you are *not* Dad. And you're not Malcolm, and you're not just a demon. You're Jasper Jones, and if you want to be with Caleb the kind-hearted bear man, you can do that."

"How?" His voice cracked pathetically.

"You said those flowers suppress our influence?"

Jasper nodded.

"Well, maybe try that? Not all the time—sounds shitty. But you're worried about Caleb's consent?"

He nodded again.

"Well, Caleb can consent to being with you, even if you're an incubus and a demon. Not everyone hates that, and we do come with some pretty cool fringe benefits." She winked. "As for the thrall thing, don't treat him like a sex doll, and he won't become one. Just . . . treat him like a person. He can make his own choices. Loving you's a pretty good one."

Jasper chewed his lip. He was still scared he'd mess up, but she kissed his cheek and pressed on.

"You're not going to be happy in Lyric anyway, Jas. It's okay. Just, maybe make him get a landline? I'll go crazy if you ditch me here with Malcolm and Dad and reclusive Declan and no word."

Jasper's mouth felt dry, but slowly, he nodded. Maybe, maybe he could do this.

Then, he was up, grabbing a leather backpack that was more for show than use, and stuffing clothes into it.

"That's my boy," Sasha said, making sure he packed his cell phone and charger and—and there wasn't really much in his room that he needed.

He pulled on jeans, a T-shirt, and a hoodie. Then he slipped his feet into his hiking boots. "Give me a ride?"

"Are you ditching your car?"

"I . . . think so. Caleb's got one, and mine's kind of over the top to sit out in the woods all the time. Don't even know how I'd charge it."

Sasha grabbed his keys, grinning. "Sweet." She hugged him tight for a second anyway.

"Do you think he'll forgive me?" Jasper whispered.

"He'd be a fool not to."

Jasper wasn't sure that was true, but he had to try anyway. He slung his backpack onto his shoulders. "I just need to make one stop on the way out of town."

He had to get some Oreos.

22

CALEB

It was probably early in the season to be chopping firewood when he had only his own small space to heat, but Caleb had some aggression to work out.

Also, he had the feeling it was going to be an especially cold winter.

He stopped to take his shirt off, wiping his sweaty face on it before tossing it aside. In the space of a few weeks, it had gone from freezing and snowy to too warm to chop wood in a shirt.

No wonder Poppy had decided it was time for him to be up for the year.

He rolled his neck in a circle to try to release some of the pent-up tension, not that it helped, and took a drink from his nearby water bottle.

Maybe he really did hate himself, but as he worked, all he could think of was, *Honestly, Jasper, you'd have been better off with the animal.*

Apparently that was how incubi saw Caleb. Less appealing than a bear. He wondered why Jasper had even bothered with him. Grateful Caleb had saved his life? Just hungry and willing to accept anything that was in front of him?

He hefted his axe and settled the piece of wood in place, and his swing went all the way through and lodged in the stump beneath. He glared at it, but that was when movement on the edge of the clearing caught his eye.

There, in all his incubus glory, stood Jasper. His adorable horns were out, eyes as red as cardinals, and pointy teeth worrying his lower lip as he stood there at the edge of the woods, watching Caleb work.

Was that the hint of a lashing tail behind him?

He was back in his hiking clothes too, and they suited him better.

What the hell was wrong with Caleb, that his first thought upon seeing a man who'd used him, wasn't interested in him, didn't even *like* him, was how fucking much he had missed him?

Jasper froze for a moment on the edge of the clearing, but eventually, he drew himself up to his full height, squared his shoulders, and stepped out of the woods.

That was when Caleb realized that Jasper had two things in his hands. A bag of Oreos and a little yellow flower.

What the hell?

He forgot all about the axe and marched over to Jasper, ready to snatch the flower away and tell him to get the fuck out of the woods, but as he approached, Jasper held out the bag of cookies.

"They're not the same ones," he admitted. "I kind of ate the ones you brought. But I got you some more."

Caleb didn't know what to say. Why the hell would Jasper bring him cookies? What did he want? Was the flower some kind of play for sympathy?

Instead of asking everything he wanted to, all he got out was, "Why?"

Jasper winced a little, but he didn't pull back. "I'm"—he motioned down at himself—"you know what I am. What my family is. My father keeps a house full of humans as sex toys. They're practically zombies. My brother doesn't take his wallet clubbing, because he knows his pheromones will convince someone to buy him whatever he wants. He came home with a Rolex once."

"You never asked me for a Rolex," Caleb pointed out. It was an inane comment, maybe, but a point that seemed important with the context.

Jasper's lips thinned into a self-deprecating grimace. "So my sister pointed out to me. That, you know, if I don't treat you like a sex doll, you won't be one."

Caleb snorted at the very idea of someone keeping him as a sex toy. Big, ungainly, furry bear fae-shifters didn't make good toys. "Wouldn't be a decent sex doll if you tried to keep me as one. No one has a Smoky the Bear doll."

Jasper rolled his eyes and huffed. "That's because they've never had you. And they all have bad taste. Bears are the sexiest and you're by far the sexiest bear."

"That guy—"

"Malcolm is an asshole," Jasper interrupted, clearly aware of the source of Caleb's doubt. "He's never had a relationship that lasted longer than one night, unless it was two nights in a row. You can hardly take his opinions seriously."

Caleb stopped and really thought about it. He missed Jasper. Was it possible the whole thing had just been bad communication? He jerked his chin in the direction of the flower. "And that?"

Jasper held the damn thing up. "The witch who told me to eat one." Poppy. Godsdammit, he was talking about Poppy. Jasper had almost died because of her. "She said if I eat one, it'll block my pheromones. You won't want me because I'm an incubus, just because I'm, you know, me—I mean, if you still do want me."

Caleb wanted to hug him and shake him in almost equal measures. "I've never wanted you because you're an incubus, you ridiculous ass."

"But—"

"I'm half fae and have the constitution of a bear, Jasper. Your powers aren't that strong."

Jasper's eyes widened in shock. "So Poppy—"

"Is my sister."

"Oh . . ."

Then he ducked his head and went back to biting his lip, so Caleb rolled his eyes and waved at the flower. "If that's what you need to convince you, then fine, eat the damn thing. And then once you're convinced, you're coming inside and drinking the cure."

Jasper flinched a little, and Caleb had a moment of guilt

because the stuff really was vile, but he sure as hell wasn't going to let Jasper be poisoned.

One more time, Jasper held out the damned disgusting cookies, and finally, Caleb took them with a sigh. "You know you're going to be the one to eat these, right? I don't even like Oreos."

Jasper's eyes went wide, and around his mouthful of poison, he hissed, "Monster!"

Caleb rolled his eyes, grabbed Jasper and slung him over his shoulder, and headed for the cabin.

23

JASPER

Jasper wished he were the kind of guy who didn't need proof. As much as he didn't want to hurt himself, though, he didn't want to hurt Caleb even more. So the flower it was.

He'd just make sure. And now that he wasn't starving and wasn't, you know, ignorantly gorging himself on poison, it wouldn't be so bad. He knew how to do it now. Trust a fae to give him half the information he needed and turn him out into the woods to figure out the rest.

Even with the poisoning, Poppy had maybe done Jasper the biggest favor of his life.

Caleb carried him into the cabin over his shoulder, giving him a view of his ass and the sheen of sweat on his bare lower back that Jasper wanted nothing more than to lick.

He bit his tongue. That could wait until he was sure Caleb not only wanted him but could forgive him.

When Caleb carried him inside, he set him on the counter by the oven. Jasper let his backpack fall to the kitchen floor and watched with his heel bouncing against the counter as Caleb dropped ingredients into a pot to simmer.

Caleb was quiet as he worked, so Jasper was startled when he broke the silence. "You wanna ask me anything?"

"I'm sorry I left you," Jasper blurted out.

Stirring the pot, Caleb just nodded. It killed Jasper that he couldn't see his eyes. "Me too."

Jasper flinched, but Caleb hadn't left him out in the clearing —he'd brought him inside. And it wasn't to torture him. He was just quiet and a little gruff. And Jasper'd hurt his feelings too. Caleb was allowed to be hurt; if Jasper loved him, it was his job to ease that feeling.

His tail flicked out and wrapped around Caleb's wrist, dragging his attention away from the simmering brew. He turned and stared at Jasper, waiting, his expression guarded in a way it hadn't been since that first day.

"I thought I was going to hurt you. And I got better, and I wanted you so much, and I was scared I'd take more than I could give back. I mean, come on, it's not like I've met another half-fae bear shifter before. I didn't know you'd be okay." He still didn't know it, but Caleb said he would. Jasper had to trust him.

Caleb grumbled, so Jasper reached out and touched his cheek. "Is it really so crazy that I might be a little formidable too?"

"No," Caleb said. Rather than imply Jasper was weak and

wilting, he smoothed his brow. "But I've known what you are. I never felt like you were trying to hurt me."

"That's what's so insidious about us—it feels good when we hurt you." In the space it took for Jasper to draw a breath, Caleb's scowl darkened and his mouth opened to argue. Jasper cut him off. "But I didn't hurt you until I left, did I?"

"No."

A small, self-depreciating laugh escaped him. "Right. So I should've talked to you instead of running off. I should've trusted when you said you loved me. Do you st—" Jasper dropped his hand, but Caleb caught it before it hit his lap. He stepped in closer, his hips pressing against Jasper's knees. His callused fingers brushed Jasper's palm in slow, soothing circles. "Could you maybe give me another chance?"

Caleb could've held it over him, could've made him squirm, but instead, he nodded. The smallest hint of a smile played at the left corner of his lips.

Jasper couldn't resist leaning in and kissing him there. Then, Caleb turned his head and caught his lips before he could pull away. His mouth was soft and sweet as ever, his skin a little salty with sweat. His tongue swept into Jasper's mouth, drawing out a moan that Caleb drank down.

His arms stretched out, wrapping around Caleb's neck and tugging him in. He used the leverage to pull himself to the edge of the counter, spreading his legs to trap Caleb between them. If he could find the right leverage—oh, there. He rocked his hips forward, rewarded when Caleb pushed against him.

Caleb's hands were on his back, under his shirt. He shivered and squirmed and needed—gods, he needed everything. He needed to mold himself to Caleb's sweaty bare chest.

"Caleb—" he rasped.

His bear chuckled against his lips. "Cure first."

Jasper whined, dropping his head so far back it thunked against the cabinet. "Fine."

Waiting for it to simmer an appropriate amount of time, then watching Caleb strain it, was agonizing. He'd missed Caleb, and if all Caleb wanted was to sit on the couch and snuggle, that'd be okay. As long as they were touching, Jasper thought he'd live. But Jasper hadn't fed since he'd left Caleb. He was hungry for more than cookies.

Once Caleb mixed in sugar and dropped in an ice cube so it wouldn't be too hot, he passed Jasper the cup. Jasper stared down into it, frowning.

"You're absolutely sure you can forgive me?" The top of the liquid shivered with the tremor in Jasper's hand. For now, nothing Caleb said would be bent by demonic lust. Before Jasper assumed this was really okay, he needed to hear it.

"Yup." Caleb tapped the bottom of the cup, inching it closer to Jasper's lips.

"And you don't mind if, I, um, stay here—for a bit?"

"I'd prefer forever, but no, I don't mind if you stay here with me." Caleb leaned in. He nudged Jasper's nose with his own "And I think your horns are cute."

"You do?"

Caleb chuckled. "I do. Now please drink that so I can stop worrying about you."

Jasper drank it in huge gulps. Even with Caleb's efforts to make it palatable, he grimaced.

Only when the cup was empty did Caleb ease it out of his hand and lean in, replacing the foul taste with a gentle brush of lips that had Jasper whimpering.

"I missed you so much," he whispered against Caleb's lips.

He could've spent hours nuzzling his cheek against Caleb's beard, familiarizing himself with the way he smelled again—so good in his memories, but nothing compared to the real thing. But Caleb slipped his hands under Jasper's ass and hauled him off the counter.

"Hungry?" Caleb asked.

Jasper groaned. "Starving."

Frowning, Caleb looked at him with concern swimming in his gorgeous eyes. For a second, Jasper worried Caleb might think he'd gone out and, well, did what incubi did. But then he realized the concern in Caleb's gorgeous eyes was just for his well-being.

Jasper flushed. "Well, you did say you were going to ruin me for everyone else."

His thighs squeezed around Caleb's hips. They kissed all the way to the bed, and when Caleb tried to tip him back onto the mattress, Jasper was loath to let him go. The only enticement was that Caleb's shirt had already been discarded outside, and if he could get out of his own clothes, he could feel the heat and press of Caleb's muscles—the tickle of his chest hair.

Jasper tumbled back, flicking the buttons of his jeans open as Caleb pulled his boots off. His pants and briefs followed seconds later, and Jasper whined as Caleb brushed his fingers softly over his thighs. It was perfect and not nearly enough. He spread his legs, shifting his hips, trying to entice him higher.

"All for me?" Caleb asked, his voice gloriously raspy as he cupped Jasper's balls. He rolled his fingers, and Jasper's cock jerked on his belly.

"Fuck, yeah. Just you. I need—"

"You need me to take care of you," Caleb growled. "Don't you, babe? Need my cock."

Jasper keened. All his pride and restraint melted away. He was so fucking hungry, and Caleb was exactly who he needed. The thought that he could have him—have this—forever was too much.

He shoved his elbow into the mattress and reached up for Caleb's shoulder. The outline of his cock was trapped in his jeans, and Jasper needed them off. He tore at the button while Caleb's hand pressed flat against his back and held him close, lifting him up like he was nothing.

He let Jasper shimmy his jeans down his hips. Trapped between their bodies, they thrust their cocks together, Jasper using his grip on Caleb's shoulders to arch his body.

"Lube," Caleb demanded. Jasper tipped over to grab it from the nightstand and slicked Caleb's fingers.

Gods, it was nice to be in the arms of a big, tall man. Caleb held him steady with one hand. His other reached around Jasper's back and down the cleft of his ass to slide one thick finger into him.

Jasper moaned. Every squirm had him rocking between the

dual pleasure of the fingers pistoning in and out of him, and the heavy heat of Caleb's huge cock.

"N—need you," Jasper stammered. "Inside. Fuck me, Caleb. Please."

He shivered at the loss of Caleb's fingers, but Caleb crawled on his knees onto the bed, kicking his jeans off on the way. He tipped Jasper back again, and then he was inside him.

He thrust in, slow and relentless, until he was fully sheathed inside him. Jasper threw his head back as Caleb rocked into him, again and again, deep and thick and grounding. For a moment, nothing mattered but that full, pounding pleasure.

With his head tipped back, he exposed the length of his golden neck to Caleb. He nuzzled into it, almost like a cat scent marking their person, and Jasper smiled.

"Mine," Caleb growled against his skin. Then he felt the scrape of his teeth, the press, and Jasper gasped, arching up.

"All yours," Jasper swore. "Every inch."

He gripped Caleb's dark hair tight. Caleb's hands clenched on his ass, dragging him up to meet every brutal thrust. When he came, Jasper's vision flashed white. His lips fell open on who knew what praises and curses. And Caleb followed swiftly after, pumping searing come into him with tiny, deep thrusts.

When Caleb caught his breath, he rolled to his side, tugging Jasper along too. With a press of his knee, Jasper lifted himself to straddle Caleb. This time, though, he just settled into his chest to listen to the race of Caleb's heart.

His hand slipped down, tracing the lines of muscle on Caleb's bicep, then his forearm. He linked their fingers together.

"I love you," he whispered.

"Love you too," Caleb said without a second's pause. Jasper's heart filled fuller than his stomach, and he turned to hide his face against Caleb's chest.

This was all too perfect. He didn't know if he deserved it, but Caleb sure as hell did. If it made him happy, Jasper wasn't going to fuck it up. Not again.

"I like that, you know," Caleb mumbled

"Fucking?" Jasper laughed.

The man rolled his eyes dramatically. "Obviously I like that, but no. It's . . . that feeling when you feed. Tingling, all knotted up in my chest. Like we're connected. It's nice."

"Oh." Jasper's lips fell slack. He wasn't sure what to say to that. He'd never thought his feeding could be good for both of them, or that Caleb felt it too. Sinking down, squeezing his hands under Caleb's shoulders in his best approximation of a hug, Jasper nuzzled his chest with his cheek. "I'm really glad."

The sound Caleb made then—as much a vibration in his chest as anything—was contented. He wrapped his arm around Jasper's back to hold him close, and his fingers traced the lines of Jasper's cheekbone, his jaw, his ear. That, too, was an absolutely wonderful tingle.

"Will you teach me to cook?" Jasper whispered after a while.

He lifted his head when Caleb shrugged. He was scowling up at him, more confused than angry. "Sure?"

"I just . . . you feed me so well. I'd like to return the favor."

A slow, broad grin split Caleb's lips, and he tugged Jasper down for another kiss.

24

CALEB

Caleb woke to the smell of sausage, and no Jasper.

As he'd learned over the months they'd been living together, the lack of Jasper's scent wasn't an indication that he'd left. It meant Jasper had gone off and eaten one of those damned poison flowers.

He didn't think Jasper was trying to hurt himself. No, he thought Jasper was already hurt, and this was him trying his best to figure out how to heal. Jasper needed to know that his incubus nature had nothing to do with Caleb wanting him. He'd been wanted, demanded, so often in his life, simply because he was the child of an incubus, that he struggled to imagine why anyone would want him for a different reason.

All Caleb could do was be there and love him just the same as always. Maybe Jasper's capacity to absorb it was a bucket with a hole in the bottom that Caleb could never fill up. Maybe in the end Jasper had to figure things out for himself, but in the mean-time, all Caleb could do was keep showing up.

He rolled out of bed and headed for the kitchen, where Jasper was plating an impressive number of breakfast sausages on one plate, and two on another. Slipping in behind him, he wrapped both arms around Jasper's waist and buried his face in his neck, nibbling his way up to his ear.

"Have I told you today that I love you?"

Jasper giggled, and the sound was surprisingly lighthearted for a day he'd eaten one of those damn flowers. "You just woke up, of course not."

"Then I'm slipping." He took the pan out of Jasper's hands and set it back on the stove, then spun him around by the hips. "You are so beautiful, sweetheart. And smart, and loving, and you make the best breakfasts."

"I fried some sausage," Jasper denied. "I haven't even started the eggs."

"Screw the eggs. I'd rather have you."

Jasper pulled a kitchen towel off his shoulder and whacked Caleb's chest with it. "Absolutely not. You have the rest of the wood to chop this afternoon if we're going to be ready for hiber-nation. The weather report says we could start getting snow this weekend."

"What if I want to spend the winter with you instead of hibernating?" Caleb couldn't lie, he was kind of starved, and the thought of a day of labor made him even hungrier. He snatched a sausage off his plate and stuffed the whole thing in his mouth.

Jasper watched him eat, always amused and somehow

beyond all reason, loving, as he watched Caleb scarf down enormous quantities of meat. "Don't be ridiculous. You're going to spend the winter hibernating *and* with me. It's not a choice."

Caleb reared back, staring at him in faked astonishment. "You mean you live here?" Jasper whacked him with the towel again, but Caleb leaned in to plant a kiss on his beautiful lips. "Sounds like I'm a pretty lucky bastard."

That made Jasper smile at him and then lean over to rest his head on Caleb's shoulder. "I don't know about lucky, but you're my favorite bastard."

Caleb left one arm wrapped around Jasper's waist and grabbed another sausage with the other, swaying their hips back and forth together. "You hungry?" he asked, and they had been together long enough that Jasper knew he wasn't offering breakfast sausage.

"This afternoon," Jasper said with a tiny shake of his head. "You have too much to do right now."

Caleb wiped his greasy fingers on the kitchen towel as he pulled it away from Jasper and set it on the counter. Then he grabbed Jasper's ass in both hands and hefted him up, pausing for a moment to let Jasper wrap his long legs around his hips.

Finally, he lifted one hand back up to caress his incubus's cheek. "Sweetheart, I never, ever have so much to do that I don't have time for you. You're what my time is for. It's everything else that's the distraction."

Jasper's eyes were wide and a little glassy. "The flowers aren't growing anymore. I grabbed the last whole one this morning."

"Good," Caleb whispered back, lips ghosting back and forth

across Jasper's. "Maybe by the time they start growing again, I'll have you convinced you don't need them. I don't give a damn if you're using your sneaky incubus powers on me. I want you this way, that way, and every other way. Every day, every way. Always."

Jasper buried his face in Caleb's neck, but Caleb didn't miss the pleased smile the words had evoked. His lips tickled Caleb's skin when he whispered, "I think maybe you could."

He kissed a line across Jasper's shoulder as he walked them over to the bed, to their little den.

"I've got days to chop wood," he told Jasper as he lay him across the bed, and pressed in immediately after him with a soft, sweet kiss. "I've only got a lifetime to spend with you. Can't waste that."

ABOUT SAM BURNS

Sam is an author of LGBTQIA+ fiction, mostly light-hearted romances. Preferably ones that include werewolves, dragons, magic, or all of the above. Most of her books include a little violence, a fair amount of swearing, and maybe a sex scene or two.

She is a full-time writer who lives in the Midwest with her husband and cat.

For more information:
www.burnswrites.com
Sam@burnswrites.com

.

ABOUT W.M. FAWKES

W.M. Fawkes is an author of LGBTQ+ urban fantasy and paranormal romance. She lives with her partner in a house owned by three halloween-hued felines that dabble regularly in shadow walking.

For more information:
www.fawkeswrites.com
waverly@fawkeswrites.com

ALSO BY W.M. FAWKES

LORDS OF THE UNDERWORLD SHORT STORIES

Heart of the Sea by W.M. Fawkes

Manufactured by Amazon.ca
Bolton, ON

24204843R00088